OUR SOULS WE KEEP

JORDAN DUGDALE

Cover artist: Fran @coverdungeonrabbit

Dedication page art: Etheric Designs

Chapter header/scene break art: Marta @marta.intotheforest

Map: Joshua Dugdale

BOOKS BY
JORDAN
DUGDALE

<u>The Whispered Tales Series</u>

The Tidings of Misfits

A Waltz Through Flames

A Song of Hope

Our Souls We Keep (companion novella)

<u>The Feyrsia Chronicles</u>

A Flower's Fatal Thorn (book one in the Rose & Moth duology)

Courting the Dragon Mage (standalone)

For those who fight for what sets their soul aflame.

Keep fighting.

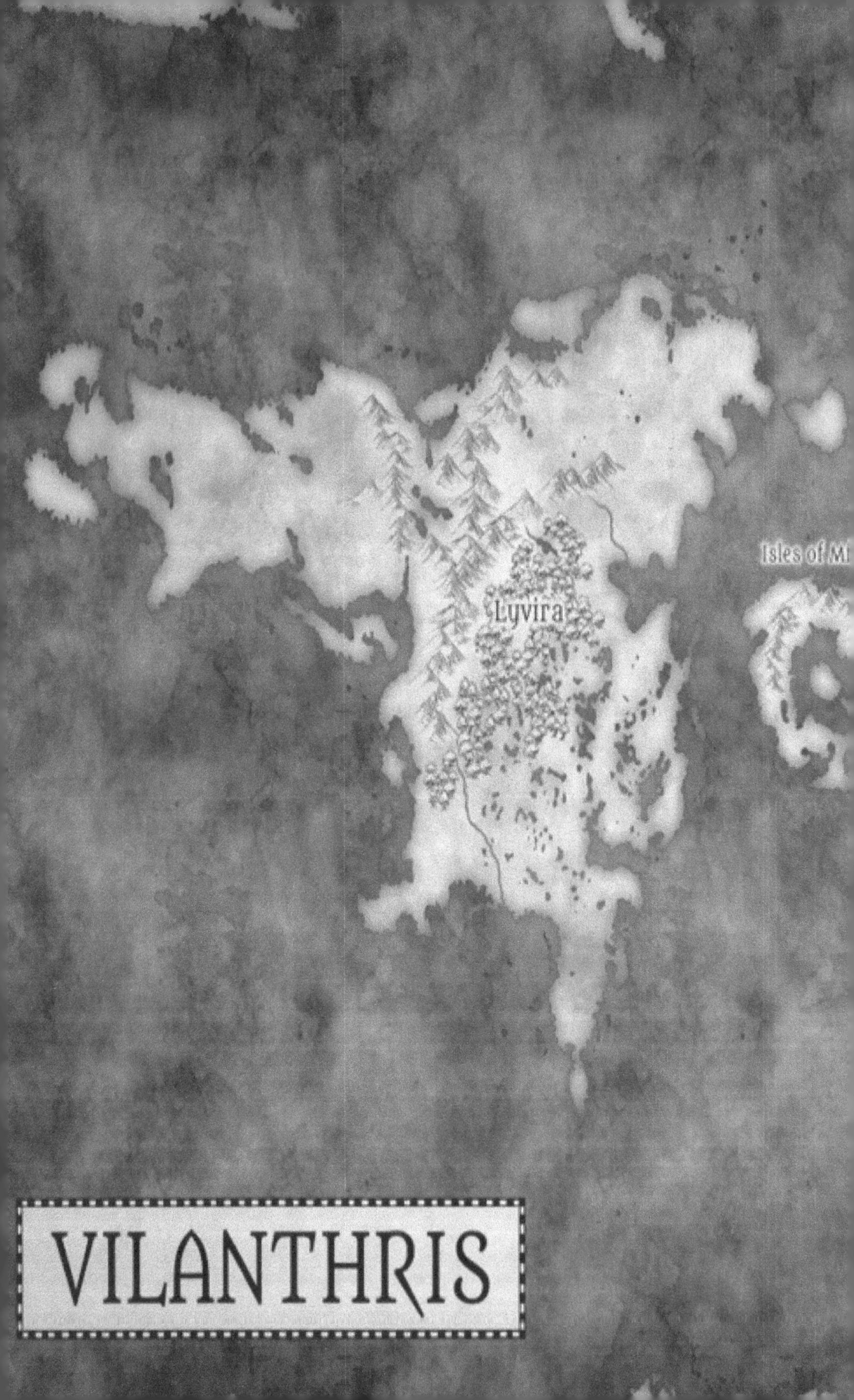

Lyvira
Isles of M[...]
VILANTHRIS

Kreznov
Volreya
Spine Mountains
Volendam
Amajin
Wolstadt
Fraheim
Nantielle
Rovania
Wilhaven
Halvdarc
Hestia
Kythera
Daesthara
Shoma
Dalasae

CONTENT WARNINGS

This title is not suitable for readers who find discomfort from the following: Cult activity (including a ritualistic sacrifice), body horror (briefly mentioned), sexual assault (briefly mentioned/involving non-consensual touching through illusion magic), very minor hints of transphobia (spoken about in passing), family trauma, torture (two scenes), and your standard fantasy violence (battles, gore, battle horror, death, murder, etc.)

WHAT CAME BEFORE...

The Tidings of Misfits

At the beginning of their journey, the vampire Cassius finds himself woken from a tomb he's been imprisoned inside of for the last five years. Fleeing back to his estate, he's only given a short time to collect himself before he discovers a magical gun has been placed inside his arm, and with it, a shadowy woman who urges him to Volendam where he may collect another piece of such magical armory.

His journey takes him through the Spine Mountains, where he is eventually captured by Shoma'kah, slavers of the sands. During his imprisonment, he meets Rooster, a human man with no recollection of his past, Helai, a woman from Shoma, and two drikoty, lizardfolk from Lyvira named Intoh and Linda.

Their journey is forever changed when they fall through a crack in the ground and land inside the mountain, where giant, mutated rats called the rakken intercept the slaver's caravans and mark the five of them with a dark brand. As they fight their way out of the mountain with the help of dwarves they meet along the way, their brand calls to something in Volendam.

After many trials, they find themselves inside the port trading city, where they meet Velius, an eldrasi blacksmith on board a ship called the Firebrand. There, he offers them aid. The only price is to infiltrate an exclusive club in the wealthy district and steal a few gems and a mysterious locket. After meeting Velius, they make their way to the nearest inn, The Broken Arrow, where they're received warmly by inn workers Felix, Patrina, and Hilde.

Meanwhile, Cassius discovers that the woman in his arm has been pulling him towards an abandoned opera house, where something calls him inside. With no weapons to speak of, Cassius refrains from entering just yet, and the ragtag team sets out to retrieve what Velius asked for to have their weapons made. They end up fighting mermaids to gain entry into the exclusive club, where they successfully retrieve the gems and locket for Velius. Upon touching said locket, Rooster has a vision of his past, and of a woman with fiery red hair. He knows it has some tie to his past so he keeps it for himself and tells Velius that it has been lost.

After receiving their newly forged weapons from Velius, they make their way to the opera house, where they discover a group of vampires standing in the way of the object Cassius has been sent to retrieve. It's a hard battle but a battle won nonetheless, and as the Misfits move to leave, they're called out to by a strange door. Inside they discover a ritual being performed by rakken and dyrvak, large woodland creatures similar to centaurs (only deer instead of horses) as they surround a dragon tooth. Their attempts to resurrect the dragon are foiled by the Misfits who stumble back out into the streets of Volendam and they discover that the city has been surrounded by an army of dyrvak and they must prepare themselves:

War is upon them.

A Waltz Through Flames

The second book in the *Whispered Tales* series opens up with a lone rakken scuttling through the sewers as he tails the Misfits from below the city of Volendam. There, he finds a small cult of rakken worshiping the dragon god Gorvayne, the same god whose sigil brands each of the Misfits. The chapter ends with that lone rakken branding himself with the same sigil, eager to find someone called *Carter*.

Above, the city of Volendam is being sieged by the horrific dyrvak, a woodland deer-centaurian race that worships the lost dragon gods. The Misfits fight valiantly to hold the city's walls, but it appears the dyrvak have teamed up with the Spine Mountain's rakken, who use their vile magic to blow up the city's walls. With the wall lost,

Cassius, Helai, and Rooster retreat to the docks, where Linda and Intoh are fighting a massive, dead deer in Volendam's bay. It is at the docks where they make their final stand and manage to keep claim over their city. But it is not without major loss, one nearly being the vampire Cassius, who narrowly survives a grievous wound. He makes his recovery on the eldrasi blacksmith Velius' ship, the *Firebrand*, where some romantic tension begins to flourish. He also gets another visit from Ahma, the daughter of Emporer Aikawa from Amajin and the woman who possesses his blood. She tells him of the next piece in the armory she is having him seek out: a cuirass in Halvdarc to the south. Halvdarc is in Rovania, the same place where Cassius' estate resides, and the brand urges them all there. They also find the Broken Arrow has been utterly destroyed but to be rebuilt with the aid of the dwarves, who had come to offer their aid during the siege. Helai receives a cryptic letter from one of her Ghosts, who claims he is in Halvdarc and wishes to speak with her. Rooster manages to secure safe passage on a trade ship that will take them to Halvdarc, and soon, the Misfits leave Volendam for the first time since they've arrived.

As they're sailing down the coast, the ship they've taken passage on is attacked by Vykra, a northern people of the bitter north that seeks to claim their ship. Much seems lost as they begin to get over-whelmed, only for their savior to be of the strangest kind: a ship of vampire pirates accompanied by a hydra, a dragon-like sea beast with several heads. Even stranger? They know Rooster, or rather, Carter Wingman. Their captain is Delroy Greaves, who speaks of cults attempting to wake a dragon in the far west, and they only have so much time to find a tome that could possibly house information on keeping it asleep. He tells the Misfits that he will be in touch as he discovers more and that they are to obtain this tome if they wish for their beloved Volendam to remain untouched. Rooster wrangles with his rediscovered name, still frustrated that his amnesia holds strong. Cassius fights with his own demons.

The rest of the trip is uneventful, and they arrive in Halvdarc to find it strange. The people of the town are nowhere to be seen, hidden away in their homes. Cassius believes the cuirass they seek is in the Welker Estate, the estate of a noble family that lives on a cliffside and is known for their flower trade. He is familiar with their adviser, who meets them at the local inn to arrange a meeting. Before his arrival, two greka come into the inn searching for Intoh, who isn't discovered purely by the fact that he is wearing his illusion ring. The innkeeper kicks the greka out, but Cassius finds them to arrange a meeting with them after Intoh agrees they could have something important to say.

The adviser arrives and agrees that a meeting could be arranged if they can find Welker's missing son, Rembrandt. The Misfits agree and spend some time looking for clues on where he might have gone, but not before meeting with the greka who sought out Intoh's company. They pledge themselves to Intoh, claiming he is a prophet of their god. After, the Misfits split up to look for trails of Rembrandt. Rooster heads to the docks, but before he can arrive, he's attacked by a cultist and saved by a strange dwarf who claims to know of Rooster's past and bears the same burning brand as the Misfits. He calls himself Rackjack, and refuses to then leave Rooster's side. On the other side of town, Cassius is forced to feed and finds a father beating a young man. Cassius saves him, and the young man, who Cassius comes to find as Itale, reveals that he noticed the young Rembrandt heading towards the town Wilhaven, which is where Cassius' estate resides. With several new companions, the Misfits set out to Wilhaven.

Rembrandt's trail leads them to a strange, abandoned winery, where they discover two grotesque women who are harvesting the blood of humans. Rembrandt is among them, and while they are successful in rescuing the young boy, Rooster is seriously injured. They rush him back to Cassius' estate, where they manage to heal him. During this time, Cassius also finds out Itale is a necromancer and needs a teacher if he is to survive the death magic.

They return Rembrandt safely to his parents. Emir and Alyse Welker are extremely thankful for their child's return and demand they host a masquerade ball in their honor. Helai accidentally runs into her Ghost, a man named Zamir, who is hiding among the servants as he attempts to seek out a lamp in Emir Welker's possession. The lamp is a jinn lamp, one capable of granting wishes. He also fills Helai in on Massoud's whereabouts and the fact that Shoma has declared war on Hestia, who have long since been at peace and in a trade agreement with one another.

The estate grows more unsettling the longer the Misfits remain, and Cassius soon finds that the cuirass he seeks is inside Emir Welker's personal collection. He will need to figure out a way to steal it before they leave.

The masquerade ball arrives, and the Misfits have a plan to steal both the cuirass and the lamp, which they found behind some magical lock in the library. Every plan falls apart as each Misfit is captured and rendered unconscious, only to wake up tied up beneath the estate. There, they are rescued by Rackjack, but in doing so he reveals himself to be a rakken. Though they've only been known as an enemy up until now, Rooster protects him, determined to know how Rackjack is linked to his past.

Emir Welker appears, and it is revealed he is a cultist of the dead dragons. They chase him to a room where cults surround a massive tooth. A woman stands before Rembrandt, who's tied to a wooden post. The Misfits are tied up, and Cassius is brought to the center of the room, where he is sacrificed, his blood smeared across the dragon tooth. A phoenix dragon is reborn; Rhavna is resurrected. In the darkness of death, Cassius speaks to Drausmírtus, the god of death. He binds himself to them and, in return, is brought back, reforged with wings and a lack of bloodlust, though his vampirism remains. Before Drausmírtus banishes Rhavna by wounding her and sending her north, she burns Rembrandt and his mother alive and eats the rest of the cultists. The Misfits then blink, and they're back at the ball, where the estate begins to burn, and they're forced to flee.

Once they get outside, they seek out Velius, whom Rackjack recognizes and calls Tantien. They seek shelter on his ship, and, using his portal, takes them back to The Broken Arrow, which has been rebuilt. A bathhouse, named in Cassius' honor, has been built, a gift from the dwarves for the Misfits' aid in the mountain all that time ago. It is then they realize two things: the brand that has been tying them together is no longer ailing them, and Velius is actually named Tantien, and he seeks the Misfits' aid in breaking his sister out of an eldrasi prison. Rooster discovers Tantien is Igraine's brother, the redhead in his memories. In order to save Igraine, they must travel south to the war-torn city of Alavae and rescue Massoud, one of Helai's ghosts. He is a master illusionist and can aid in the coming prison break.

<u>A Song of Hope</u>

The third book in the *Whispered Tales series* begins in Massoud's POV as he infiltrates a Shoman camp on the edge of Alavae, a Hestian city being sieged by the Shoman army. Massoud finds himself in one of the general's beds in attempt to spy and gather information for the Alavaen troops, but is discovered and thus captured and tortured for information.

The first chapter opens with the Misfits in the Broken Arrow Inn, where they prepare to sail to Alavae to locate Massoud. Rooster has just discovered information about his past and its tied to Tantien's sister, Igraine, who is imprisoned on the eldrasi island of Míradan. They hope to seek out Massoud, a lost friend of Helai's, in hopes that his talent in illusion magic can help aid them in breaking Igraine out of prison.

Tantien sails them down to Alavae. On the way down, Cassius and Tantien share an intimate moment that ultimately leads to Tantien's rejection. Tantien is looking for casual moments, where Cassius longs for companionship. They leave on relatively good terms, however, and the city of Alavae approaches before too long, where the Misfits are immediately thrust into the heart of battle.

As they sail to shore, Helai and one of her Shoman friends, Zamir, fight side by side as they all attempt to get to the front gate of the city.

Intoh is the only one to stay behind on the ship with Tantien, hopeful he can aid them in the sea battles that are approaching. Everything seems to be going well until a Shoman soldier manages to cut down Zamir and Helai nearly loses hope. It is her determination to find Massoud that urges her forward, and the rest of the Misfits manage to make it to the city, where they are led to Angelica, one of the Alavaen generals.

There, they learn several things: a Shoman general is in the catacombs just outside the city and needs to be dealt with and Massoud has been captured by the enemy. From here, the Misfits split into two teams – Helai and Linda sneak out to rescue Massoud, and Cassius, Rooster, and Rackjack head to the tombs of Alavae to deal with the other general.

Helai and Linda manage to make their way through the Shoman camp, where Massoud is being tortured over an open flame. Whip marks mar his back, and after killing the general, Massoud dies. Helai uses the djinn lamp she's been carrying all this time to bring him back, and we do not yet know what the price is for her wish. Her and Linda separate as Linda attempts to return to the city, where they run into Drithan, the dwarf from Obrand's company. Linda gets a vision from one of the gods of their people, and can now breathe fire at will. Meanwhile, Cassius and co learn that the general in the catacombs is attempting to open a portal for rakken to flood the city, and they have to deal with him and a djinn of their own as they narrowly accomplish it. Rooster nearly dies and Rackjack loses a leg, but they manage to kill the general and free the djinn, only to slowly return to the main part of the city. Intoh deals with a djinn as well with Tantien as a naval battle breaks out, and they only succeed due to the arrival of Delroy, the vampire pirate, and his hydra companion.

After the generals fall, Alavae is deemed victorious as they temporarily push back the Shoman forces. From there, the Misfits travel to Míradan. During their travels, Cassius and Massoud share a few romantically tense moments, and the Misfits figure out their plan to infiltrate the prison to free Rooster's crew and Tantien's sister. Upon arriving at Míradan, much occurs. Their presence is discovered after Rooster meets with a witch to get more information on the prison and Igraine's location. The Misfits are attacked at the inn they're staying at by the city guard, where one of the greka traveling with the Misfits is killed. They manage to escape and make it to the city where the prison is located. From there, they do two things: they go to the city's equivalent of a museum, where they steal an artifact capable of keeping gods asleep per Delroy's request, and then they perform their heist in the prison. They manage to break Rooster's crew out of prison, and as they are escaping, Rooster steals a lamp Helai had plucked off the Shoman general in Alavae and uses it to blow up the prison. The book ends with them sailing to Vitreuse, a small island that is a safe haven for the Misfits, where Rooster and Igraine share an intimate evening in some hot springs, Cassius and Massoud share an intimate evening on the beach, and the Misfits find momentary reprieve from their quest to stop the dragon gods from waking.

ONE
ITALE

When Itale dreamed, it was of winter and the end of the world.

A crawling white stretched before him, frigid and un-relenting as the snow pierced his skin. His feet were frozen in the snow, and he cowered in terror as a black dragon rose before him, a great and terrible beast that promised wrath and ruin as it opened its jaw and purged its throat of fire. Beside him was a phoenix-dragon, *the* phoenix-dragon, her feathers a blinding red against the snow as she hovered beside the dragon. That *had* to be Rhavna, the dragon resurrected beneath the Welker Estate.

Close your eyes, Itale thought, as the snow burned away and the sky was swallowed up by the dragon. *It's not real. It's not real—*

"Itale?"

Itale woke suddenly in the safety of his room on the Perseverance. The ship was docked at the island of Vitreuse. Though the brightness of the sun poked through the round window above his head, the chill of the nightmare still sank heavily in his arms as he rose, his disorientation sending the room spinning. He clutched the side of his face and stilled, his attempts to ground himself only partially successful. Only when he was able to feel in control of his own body did he look to the source of whoever called his name.

Cassius stood stoically in the doorway, arms folded across his broad chest. The vampire looked strange without his armour on, his shoulder-length hair ruffled. He looked particularly human, though Itale sensed the presence of death that clung to his soul.

"Tantien has called for a meeting and told me to come and fetch you."

"Is it about the next moves?" Itale scrambled anxiously from his bed and ran his hand through the unruliness of his curls. It felt like they had just arrived at the safe haven of this island, and now they were talking about leaving it for the next danger. The weight of his nightmare bore heavily against his mind, and his stomach flopped nervously as Cassius nodded.

"I believe so. Delroy spoke to Tantien of something in the north that may be useful to our cause." The tone in Cassius' voice was light, lighter than it had ever sounded, and he remained in the doorway as Itale bustled about the room, doing what little he could to make himself presentable. He still wasn't used to being around people of importance. His father had been in such circles, but he never allowed Itale to accompany him. "It is also time to discuss about the plans going east."

The implications of Cassius' words sent another chill through Itale. It hadn't been but a few days since they had fled the prison on the eldrasi island of Míradan with a book that was thought to put a god back to sleep. One of the dragons was waking in Lyvira, one of the big ones, and its resurrection would only further the threat of the end of days. The core group of the Misfits had been discussing sailing the Perseverance east with some of the others to stop it.

Itale loathed to think of what kind of world that would bring. The dragon from his nightmare haunted him, and he stepped up to Cassius as he exhaled sharply. "Okay, I'm ready." Patting down the wrinkles on his shirt, his nerves forced a bounce in his step as he followed Cassius out of the room and towards the deck, where a small rowboat awaited them to take them to shore. The sun was bright, the ocean calm and twinkling merrily below as the rowboat was lowered and Cassius rowed them to shore. As they neared the beach, Itale startled when Linda popped out of the water, sparkles of sunlight-infused water droplets trailing off their scales as they waded towards the beach. The krok'ida was in their true form, as they had been as of late, and Itale was glad for it. It was good to see them refuse to shy away from their true self any longer; the ring that had once hidden them behind a human facade no longer gleamed against their finger. The other reptilian of the group, however, sat sheathed behind his human illusion beneath the shade of a palm tree, his blond hair tugged back into a messy ponytail. The other two members of the main Misfits, Helai and Rooster, were nowhere to be seen.

"Hi, Linda," Itale said warmly as Linda pushed themself up. They loomed over Itale, their crocodilian maw parted as they shook water from their scales, and the smile that breached Itale's lips was a genuine one.

"Itale." Linda reached out and patted Itale on the head as they helped Cassius drag the rowboat up to shore and allowed Itale to step out without getting his pants wet. "Here for meeting? Eager to go. Ready for combat again."

"So soon?" Itale teased. "You just got done fighting several battles, Linda." Itale had been away with Tantien and his crew. At the same time, the Misfits broke Rooster's crew out of prison on the island of Míradan. Still, he'd heard of the battle barely won on the shores of Alavae and was thankful he'd been stuck on the deck of the Firebrand. Tantien hadn't found whatever it was he was looking for, but Itale was glad to spend time away from the threat of battle. It seemed as though peace was about to shatter.

"Taking combat away from Linda would be like taking you away from your tea, Itale. It is in their blood," Cassius retorted, earning an agreeable snort from Itale. He couldn't recall ever seeing Linda without their war hammer, and was glad to have them on his side. He'd never met a krok'ida before Linda, but had heard of the race's fearsome nature. Linda stood as a tall example of that.

Linda shrugged. "Nothing better than fighting someone worthy in battle. What else could make heart sing?"

"A beautiful piece of poetry or song. A piping hot cup of tea. A quiet sunrise over this beautiful ocean," Itale said, tapping his fingers as he rattled off examples. "There is much beauty in the world aside from battle, Linda, if you know where to look for it."

Cassius pressed a hand to Itale's shoulder as they walked further up the shore. Linda had trailed off to speak to Sígrun, Rooster's gunnery sergeant on the Perseverance. The beach was awash with slow-moving sailors and those still asleep, bottles of empty rum at their feet as they slept away their hangovers from too much celebration the days prior. Rooster and Igraine stumbled out of the forest, looking rumpled and as if they had enjoyed each other's company the night before. Itale's cheeks blossomed with a blush at the intimate smile Igraine flashed Rooster's way. His eyes darted away before they felt his stare, settling on Tantien and Delroy as they stood near a bonfire that had long since gone out, leaving behind nothing but charred wood and smoke. A soft breeze trailed the air, and Itale inhaled the sea salt as anyone with title or importance settled near Tantien. The eldrasi had his hair tied back, highlighting the metal earrings that glinted against pointed ears. He wore a loose white linen shirt and black pants that cut off at the knee, and his hammer was absent from his side as he smiled brightly at the approaching Misfits. Helai was the only one of the Misfits who was absent.

"Sorry to pull you into a meeting so bright and early, but I'm afraid Delroy has news that can't wait."

The vampire stood beneath the shade of a tree where the sun could not pierce his dark skin, and his eyes gleamed red as he smiled, his fangs sharp and wicked. Other than Cassius, Delroy and his crew were the only vampires Itale had ever interacted with, and surprisingly, they did not make him as nervous as he had anticipated. Perhaps it was their ties to death that spoke to his own necromancy, but Itale's courage had forged stronger bonds since he'd joined the Misfits and their journeys. Though unlike Cassius, who kept himself fed and tucked behind the illusion of humanity, the pirate captain Delroy did not care to hide the monstrosity of the vampiric curse; decay puckered at his cheeks, baring a bit of bone and muscle beneath withered skin. Locs adorned his face, long and twisted, with red cloth beads decorating them in various spots beneath his dark hat.

"I have sources saying da Phoenix Mother Rhavna is in da north." A collective shudder echoed throughout the Misfits.

"It's been quite some time since we've heard news of her. Are we sure your sources are reliable? She was not in good health after she was brought back and banished by the god of death." It was Rooster that broke the silence, his arm slung across Igraine's shoulders. "If we are to travel to Lyvira, it would be a fool's errand to go north only to discover your sources are lacking."

Delroy's gaze was haunting as he turned to Rooster. Still, Rooster seemed unaffected by the intimidating nature of the vampire as he held his gaze until Delroy's smile returned. "How many phoenix dragons do you know, boy? When someone sees one flying dem frigid skies, it's pretty damn clear what we be up against." Delroy stepped forward, taking care to catch the stare of everyone surrounding him. "I aim t' travel north. Der are rumors dat one of Ulfric Ironfang's infamous daggers 'as been found, and if dat's da case, we cannot let it fall into enemy hands."

The name was unfamiliar to Itale, but Sígrun's eyes widened at Delroy's words, her mouth pressed into a thin line as she stepped forward. Vykra, by nature, demanded attention, and Sígrun was no different. She was tall and broad, her raven hair pulled back into intricate braids. Her eyes, a bright and unyielding blue, were brutal and unforgiving. "Ulric Ironfang was welcomed in the halls of his ancestors long ago. His daggers were lost to the snow. That's impossible."

"Who is Ulfric Ironfang?" Linda asked. "Fearsome warrior?"

Sígrun nodded. "He is legend. He was said to have tamed and ridden a God-Child, a massive white wolf whose howl called forth the coming of winter. My people pray to him for strength before battle." She waved her hand at Delroy. "The dagger he speaks of is said to be a fang from his wolf's own mouth and strong enough to pierce the flesh of gods."

"In da hands of da enemy, it could accomplish wicked t'ings. T'ings long forgotten in da snow," Delroy said. "We must not let dem have it."

Itale trembled. There were many things he longed to ask; they edged the tip of his tongue, but he kept silent, his nervous nature outweighing his curiosity. The northmen of Volreya, Sígrun's people, had always been closest to the gods. It was why they were so often tempted by the whispering of the dragons.

"If the dagger has truly been found, or if my people are searching for it for Rhavna, then Delroy is right. We cannot let it get into their hands," Sígrun said.

"No, we cannot, but we also cannot forget our task in Lyvira." Cassius' words sent a murmur of agreement around the group, and Itale rose his chin as the morning breeze tousled his curls.

"No," Tantien murmured, stepping forward. "Which is why the Firebrand and I will accompany Delroy. We'll handle the threat in the north while the Perseverance and the Misfits go east."

"I want to come too," Itale said before he could stop to consider it. Something inside him urged him to go with Tantien instead of the Misfits, and he recoiled slightly as all eyes turned to him, his expression turning sheepish. "I-I mean if you'll have me. I don't want to intrude, but—"

"No," Tantien said, grinning. "I think it's a wonderful idea. It's always good to have a necromancer on our side and we could use your magic to fight against the inevitable dangers we'll be facing. If the Misfits have no need for you in Lyvira, then I see no issue with you staying on the Firebrand."

Itale stilled the tremble in his fingers, driven by adrenaline. The journey north would be dangerous, something he was becoming all too intimately familiar with, but so would have been traveling east with the other Misfits. His dream lay fresh in his mind, and he knew if the Phoenix Mother woke the dragon in the north, the consequences would be catastrophic.

"Tantien...be careful." Igraine and Tantien shared a look, a look that transcended the topic at hand, and Tantien gave a vague nod in his sister's direction before clapping his hands together.

"There is much to be done, then, if we are to sail north. Much to prepare for."

"Does this mean we have to begin preparations as well?" Rooster scowled, his lower lip stuck out in a dramatic pout as he sighed and ran his hand through his hair. "I suppose it was too much to hope for more time."

"Unfortunately, the threat of evil does not wait," Cassius said, stepping over to one of the sleeping sailors to gently kick at his foot to wake him. "And it is not a short sail to Lyvira, especially if the wind does not favor your sails. We should talk about departing as soon as the coming morn."

"About time," Linda growled as Itale moved towards Tantien. "Too idle."

"Are you certain you wish to travel with us north?" Tantien asked as Itale drew close. "I would understand your desire to be near Cassius and the other Misfits."

Itale gave a soft shake of his head as he met the eldrasi's imploring gaze. "No, I'm certain I'm going where I need to be."

TWO
ITALE

As they sailed further and further from the Misfits, Itale's anxiety peaked.

He'd grown quite fond of them. So long ago was the day Cassius had ripped his father away from his beaten body. So long ago was the day of living in the shackles of his life, living in his father's shadow for fear of what he would do should he speak out of line.

A shiver rolled through him. He owed much to the Misfits for welcoming him into their little family. Did he make the right choice by following Tantien north? What if something happened to the Misfits during their time in Lyvira, and he abandoned them on a fool's errand to locate the Phoenix Mother?

These were regrets and wonders that he shoved away as Tantien barked out orders from above. The Firebrand had flourished to life as sailors went about their duties, and they sailed seamlessly through the waves. They'd left before sunrise, but now it crested over the horizon, drenching the sky in beautiful colors of pink and orange. There was still warmth in the air as sea foam brushed up against Itale's cheeks, and he clung to the railing of the ship as they dipped with the waves.

"Captain wants me to show you to your room," a voice said from behind him. Itale turned, greeted by a pretty little wisp of an eldrasi with short, dark hair and large, green eyes. Her ears were tapered to points, as all eldrasi's were, but hers were jagged as they ended in the sharpness of tree bark. When she smiled, each of their teeth was pointed.

"Of course," Itale said, taking one last look at the island Vitreuse before it disappeared over the horizon. *Until next time, Misfits.*

Following the eldrasi below deck, he found himself full of nervous energy. He'd traveled with Tantien once already while the Misfits were on the island of Míradan, but something felt different about this journey. More perilous. Full of promise should they succeed, or consequence should they fail.

"Thank you," he said as the eldrasi led him into a small room. It was nothing to speak of, but more than Itale had expected. He was surprised to find himself in a private room at all; he had expected to sleep with the crew. Instead, Tantien had put him up in a room with an actual bed and a small table, which, he thought gleefully, he could enjoy his daily tea.

"I'll leave you to get comfortable," the eldrasi said before leaving him alone. He didn't have much to unpack, not much that survived his recent travels anyway, save for his tea set and a bundle of clothes rolled up into a backpack that he set on the bed. Still, he carefully unwrapped his tea set from the safety of his clothes and put it on the windowsill, where it would be safe. As safe as they would be on a ship anyhow. Several times they rattled against their saucers, and Itale frowned. What a shame it would be if they broke. It was his favorite set.

"Settling in alright then?" A voice floated from the door, and Itale startled, turning.

Tantien leaned against the doorway of the room, arms folded over his broad chest. There was an easygoing smile tugging at his lips, his blue eyes bright as the sun shone through the small, round window behind Itale's head. The rays struck Tantien's hair, aflame in brilliant, dark red, and Itale's mouth dried. He hadn't been able to deny it for a while, how beautiful Tantien was. It made Itale painfully aware every time they were alone, and Tantien tilted his head, his smile radiant as his lips parted to reveal gleaming teeth.

"Wha—oh," Itale said, cheeks flushed in embarrassment. "I apologize. Were y-you saying something?" *Get it together, you silly boy.*

Tantien laughed lightly and pushed off the door frame, righting himself. "I was just saying that this is where Cassius stayed during the few times he boarded my ship. I thought it would be fitting for this room to be yours, considering the bond the two of you share."

Itale glanced about the room, trying to picture Cassius sitting at the table or sleeping in the bed. It was difficult to imagine the vampire doing anything so mundane. Still, there was a strange comfort that came from being where he once was. Cassius had been there for him where no one else had. He owed that man his life.

"It's cozy," Itale said, patting the back of the chair next to him with his palm. "I think it'll be perfect for me. All I need for a good living is a place to have my tea and somewhere to sleep. These supply both." His smile matched Tantien's, and his heart jumped when Tantien winked at him.

"Excellent! I'll leave you to it. Just wanted to pop in and make sure everything was fine. We should be smooth sailing for a while. Delroy's presence should keep the threat of pirates at bay."

"Tantien?" Itale called out for him as he moved to leave, and he glanced back through the doorway, his fingers curled around the door frame. "Are you sure we have any right to succeed?" Itale's laugh was nervous as he reached up to weave his fingers through the curls at the nape of his neck. A gesture to calm his anxiety, he'd come to find. "I-I mean, I know we've gone up against such gods before, but... we can't really kill a god, can we?"

"The Phoenix Mother is no god," Tantien said slowly. "Merely the general of one. Still," the hesitation and fear in his eyes preyed on Itale's own nervous nature, but it was gone so quickly, perhaps Itale might have imagined it. "Everything can die, Itale. Surely you know that better than anyone. We just need to find the right weapon. A weapon that can kill gods."

"And you really think this...dagger is that weapon?" Itale asked, his voice hushed as if he feared the very gods they spoke of would hear them.

"I don't know," Tantien admitted. "Even the first of my people who fought the dragons when they were great beasts that walked the earth in their mortal flesh could not kill them—not truly. Could be there is no such weapon." A chill ran through the room, and Itale suppressed the urge to shiver. "Something whispers in the north, though. It's our duty to Vilanthris to find out if it's possible."

"Join me for tea?" Itale changed the subject, eager to be rid of the conversation about god killing weapons and the gods themselves. The goddess of death whispered to him at times in his dreams, the darkness of their skeletal gaze ever stripping him away until his soul was bare before them. Still, Drausmírtus' voice was a comfort in the times Itale needed it. Rhavna and the god she sought to serve were not.

"Afraid there are too many duties to attend to." Tantien's smile was apologetic. "Next time."

He left, and while Itale would have enjoyed Tantien's company, there was a part of him that was glad for the alone time. Perhaps there would be many quiet days in this room with nothing to occupy his time but a good book and a cup of tea.

THREE
ITALE

They had been traveling for three days before Itale felt well enough to leave his room. Seasickness took no prisoners, and by the time he stopped lurching, nothing was coming up but the water he forced himself to drink. He'd tried everything, from the crackers the cook had on hand to lying in a hammock one of the crewmates had so graciously loaned him during the day. Nothing worked but time, and by the morning of the third day, he gained enough courage to brave the open sea air of the main deck.

Eldrasi were hard at work as Arlaynia barked orders from the top deck, where Tantien lazily operated the wheel. The red in his hair gleamed brighter against the backdrop of the sea, and Itale shielded his eyes with his hand as he peered up.

"Feeling better?" Tantien called down, an arrogant smile pressed to his lips.

"No thanks to you," Itale called up to him, unable to keep his own smile from tugging at his mouth.

Tantien's laughter echoed out, and Itale turned away to stumble to the side of the ship. He still hadn't gotten his sea legs yet, and envied the eldrasi around him who walked the deck as if they were on land. The sea was calm today, the sun bearing down and warming his head.

"Do not let the captain tease you too much—it took me *ages* to get my seasickness under control." The eldrasi that had shown Itale to his room sidled up beside him, their smile meek. "The name's Yumai. I apologize for not introducing myself before."

Itale returned the smile. "No need to apologize. It's nice to meet you, Yumai. How long have you worked for Tantien?"

Yumai's eyes lit up. "Just some months now. I was being treated poorly on a trade ship. He showed me a better life." Their voice sounded far off, as if they were reliving some memory, and they shook their head and gestured for Itale to follow. "Come. If you're going to be around for a while this time, you might as well meet the rest of the crew."

A strange feeling sat in Itale's belly, the same feeling that plagued him when he joined the Misfits: a sense of belonging. A sense of home. Cultists and the end of the world be *damned*. He'd fight for this feeling as long as he had air in his lungs.

"'os th' new guy?"

Yumai had spent the entire morning parading Itale around the Firebrand and introducing him to every crew member aboard. He hadn't bothered to do this the first time he'd spent time aboard the Firebrand, certain it would be his last. It felt right this time, though.

Yumai knew the name of *everyone*, and Itale had already come to terms with the fact that he'd never remember. They'd finally saved the lookout guy for last, a myrlír who took his job in the crow's nest very seriously. His face was too small, his ears too large, and his yellow-green skin was covered in small burn scars from the sun.

"This is Itale. He's with the Perseverance crew, but cap'n wanted him with us for this mission. You remember...the necromancer?"

The myrlír's eyes lit up as he took a long swig of his flask and then reached out, grabbing Itale's hand and shaking it violently. "Name's Yír. Tell me, tell me... d'you feel ghostly spirits all the time, or just when you're using your necromancy?"

Itale laughed nervously at the imploring questions and the myrlír's heightened energy, and Yumai frowned and swatted at Yír's shoulder.

"Let the man breathe."

"It's okay, Yumai. I don't mind." Itale gave a soft smile. "I feel them all the time, but it's like..." Itale paused, attempting to find the right words. "Like a breeze in the air or knowing someone else is in the room with you, even when your back is turned." It was quieter at sea, with the vast ocean swallowing up the soft whispers of the dead, but Itale had grown sensitive to the noise since tapping into his necromancy.

"Come — let's teach Itale how to play Weaver's Dice instead of pestering him on dealings with the dead." Yumai had wandered over to some of the other crew members (Itale had already forgotten their names) as they settled in a circle, each shaking cups full of dice. The temptation to learn had Itale drawing forward, only to startle when a hand came to rest upon his shoulder. Glancing up, Itale's gaze caught the blazing blues of Tantien's, and his stomach plummeted. One could get lost in the sea-storm of Tantien's gaze.

"Actually, I need to steal Itale away for a moment or two." Tantien's tone was lighthearted, but Itale's heart pattered nervously regardless.

"To talk about the plan forward?" Itale asked as he followed Tantien. They seemed to be heading towards the doors below the wheel, which led to Tantien's forge and room. A hefty wind howled across the deck, and Itale's hand lurched out to steady himself, a silent curse forged between his lips. He smiled sheepishly when his fingers curled against Tantien's shirt at his waist, and Tantien tossed an easygoing smile over his shoulder.

"Steady. Don't worry, you'll get your sea legs yet."

Itale frowned and inhaled sharply. "Let's hope so or I'll be as useless as I was last time you ferried me away on this ship."

Tantien barked out a laugh, brushing his hair from his eyes. "Useless would never be a word I'd use to describe you, Itale."

Heat seeped through Itale's cheeks as Tantien held the door open for him. They shuffled through, and Itale inhaled sharply as the heat of the forge pressed against his skin. He was always cold; the longer he learned and wielded his necromancy, the more it seemed to sap the warmth from him, so the forge was a welcome sight as Tantien sidled up next to Delroy, who stood several feet from Tantien's gryphon.

Kalíra shuffled his feathers as the vampire drew closer, the piercing amber of his eye critical as he clicked his beak rapidly in warning.

"You love to torment him so, Delroy. Leave my friend alone." While Tantien's tone remained lighthearted, Itale sensed the undercurrent of warning hinted in his words.

Delroy flashed a fanged smile. The vampire was nothing like Cassius Antonia, the only other vampire Itale had met. His presence demanded attention as he sauntered away from Kalíra.

"Why did you call me here, Tantien? We are at least a week's away from our destination, and only if the wind's favor us."

Tantien held up his hand in a mock surrender. "I only wish to further iron out our plans once we arrive. Rhavna is the general of a god—it would be foolish to go after her or a weapon that could kill her without a plan."

"You sail north with no plan on what you're going to do once you get there?" The accusation left Itale's lips unbidden, and he suppressed a shudder when Delroy's dark eyes fell upon him and two other vampires materialized from the shadows. Their steps were silent, their eyes glowing a vague red as one floated over to stand next to Delroy. At the same time, the other approached Itale, her smile wickedly revealing her fangs. She said nothing, but her stare was disarming, one that swallowed Itale up as she approached. He thought she might reach out and touch him as her fingers rose, only for him to startle when a hand *did* come down to rest almost lazily upon his shoulder. When he glanced up, Tantien stood behind him, his face free of emotion as he tilted and nodded. The vampire bared her teeth and retreated, and Itale released a breath he didn't know he'd been holding, his relief immense. Tantien did not remove his hand from Itale's shoulder, and heat rolled off the eldrasi in waves, tempting Itale to lean back into him, despite his necromancy recoiling at the very life magic that encompassed Tantien.

"Itale brings a good point, Delroy. We have no plan and have been following blindly since we left Vitreuse. Do we know if the weapon that can kill Rhavna has been located already, or do we have a chance of obtaining it before the enemy does?"

Delroy dragged a long fingernail across one of the tables of the forge, studying the weapons that littered the surface from Tantien's work. Some of the blades glowed vaguely, a soft green, and all were forged with a skillful hand as Delroy plucked a dagger from its spot and studied it intently before flashing it at Itale and Tantien.

"My source sent word a fortnight ago and I have since lost contact. I 'ave reason t' believe he 'as been... apprehended. We must assume the weapon has already been taken by Rhavna's cults."

Itale stilled. "If the enemy has the weapon, then what hope do we have getting there in time to stop them?"

Delroy's gaze settled on Itale, his red eyes leering. "We 'ave to hope we can get to dem before they do whatever it is dey plan ta do with it. The weapon in Rhavna's hands won't stop at bringing back lesser dragons, but da scaly gods demselves."

A chill slunk through the forge at the mention of the god general. The Misfits had witnessed Rhavna's resurrection beneath the Welker's estate, where Cassius had been sacrificed to bring her back. Had the goddess of death not intervened, Cassius would still be dead. Rhavna's return had spurred on motions to awaken Gorvayne, the dragon god of war, and killing her would certainly slow such efforts.

"We will need to be quick, then. If her cultists already have the weapon, they will be more dangerous than we originally thought," Tantien said.

Delroy sneered as he dropped the dagger back onto the table. The noise clattered about the forge, but no one flinched as Delroy turned to one of the other vampires and spoke quickly to him in a language Itale did not understand. The vampire vanished in a plume of dark shadow as Delroy reached up to stroke his beard.

"Da Misfits are in more danger of failing in Lyvira den we are. I wouldn't lead us into da north if I didn't trust da word of my source or the will of our crew. We know Rhavna is capable of being killed because it's already happened once before. We cannot afford t' leave her unchecked and unchallenged and if we can get da dagger from her cults ta stab her with, all da better."

Tantien's hand slid off Itale's shoulder as he stepped forward, a soft sigh passing his lips. "Then it must be done. No matter the cost." His hand slipped through his hair as he swept it from his face, and Itale suppressed another shiver as it rolled down his spine. Itale couldn't place it, but speaking of Rhavna seemed to manifest her will, and Itale was recalled back to the Welker Estate and the masquerade that had been going on while her resurrection occurred beneath the floors. He remembered when the music had taken a darker tune and the ghosts of the estate mingled with those of the living, their spectral bodies twirling around the dance floor as unspeakable horrors were committed beneath their feet. The forge felt the same now as it did then, and Itale glanced around, half expecting ghosts to haunt the walls of the Firebrand as well. No such spirits presented themselves, and his hands shook. He longed for a cup of tea to settle his nerves. He loathed speaking of the Old Gods.

"I understand our shaky past, Tantien Kindroth, but if we are going to sail into da enemy's territory, den we need ta be able t' trust each other." Delroy's annoyed nature had dissipated, and the other vampire had vanished, leaving the three of them alone in the forge. Had she been there at all? Itale hadn't sensed her departure and wouldn't have been surprised if illusion magic was at play. He knew some vampires were capable of it.

"I've always been a trusting man, Delroy." Tantien's smile was disarming, a wolf in sheep's clothing. "We will follow your lead, Delroy. Chart us our path, and we will not be far behind."

Delroy bowed his head and then disappeared in a flurry of screaming bats as the clouds sailed by the space where Tantien's gryphon usually resided, leaving Itale and Tantien alone in the forge.

"Well..." Itale wasn't sure what to say or how to approach their task ahead. Fear bred itself in the air, stitched against his skin like an unwanted companion. "Do you think we stand a chance?"

Tantien shook his head and focused on Itale, his signature soft smile curling warmth into Itale's belly. "The odds are probably against us, I'm afraid, but that hasn't stopped us before."

Itale's laugh was nervous as he reached up to grab a fistful of his hair. "True. And if we don't find it, who will?"

Tantien's eyes darkened as he turned back towards the forge door. "The enemy, and we cannot allow that to happen. As Sígrun said back on Vitreuse, Ulfric Ironfang is of the legends, and his weapons hold immeasurable power. It does not come as a surprise to me that it's one of his weapons we seek. Come. I believe my crew wanted to introduce you to Weaver's Dice." Throwing a smile over his shoulder, Tantien barked out a laugh. "Good luck trying to beat Yír. The myrlír has a nasty habit of being excellent at the game."

Itale's laughter joined Tantien's as he followed the eldrasi out onto the main deck. It calmed Itale's anxieties about what lay ahead, but a nagging fear persisted, warning him that danger was coming.

FOUR
ITALE

Blood spilled across the deck, an ugly, stark color as Itale tucked himself behind the safety of a round barrel and wiped his hair from his face. The salt of the sea air was thick on his tongue as another vyrka swung from their ship to the Firebrand, where they were immediately met with eldrasi resistance. Itale had been foolish to think they were safe after calm seas for a week. The Vykra had come out of nowhere.

"Show them no mercy," Tantien seethed as he brushed past Itale, his eyes blazing with rage. No mercy was given, not to any of the Vykra that came aboard. Not that Itale thought they deserved it. They spoke of wicked things anytime he was near enough to hear them.

He shuddered as he forced his nerves to still. Cassius would have been proud of him. He'd come far from the scared boy being beaten by his father in the streets. So far that when he raised his hands and beckoned his magic forth, he didn't even hesitate, and it came to him easily and with familiarity, intimate as a lover.

Necromancy was strange, like the cold whisper of breath against the back of the neck at night, or the tension that bled in the air when something was wrong. It was the strange *wrongness* that settled against the skin, only for Itale? It was natural. Right. Comforting. He never knew how he had lived so long without it.

"A little help," Tantien called back, his voice tinged in exasperation as he slammed his hammer into the face of a Vykra, whose head cracked back so harshly the sound carried across the ship as the northman crumbled to the ground.

Itale lurched forward, reaching out through the energies of magic in the air to pluck the strings of the Vykra that had just fallen. The body twitched, so Itale plucked harder, his mouth set in a determined line as he pried the corpse up into a standing position, animated and ready to obey his will. He sent it crashing into another Vykra who'd managed to sneak up behind Tantien, sword poised and at the ready, and they both fell to the ground, where Tantien killed the living Vykra with reckless abandon.

Itale brought that one back, too. And then another. And another.

Sweat dripped from his brow as he trembled, the strings of magic tied to each corpse he brought back taut against his extended fingers. The reanimated corpses moved slowly, their movements twitchy as they aided the eldrasi in pushing the Vykra back. The fight was over almost as quickly as it had begun, and Itale slumped away, releasing his magic as several corpses fell, dead again, to the deck of the ship. One Vykra moved to throw himself at Tantien, but one of the sailors struck him down, his sword poised to kill.

"Wait," Tantien barked. "Keep that one alive. Take him to the brig." Several sailors strode forward, tugging the leering Vykra to his feet and dragging him away.

"Third one this week?" Itale asked, forcing his breath to even. Necromancy was strenuous, more strenuous than he was used to, and no amount of sleep had caught him up on just how taxing the death magic was.

Tantien strode past him, his hair plastered against his face as he spoke quickly and quietly to an eldrasi sailor in eldrasian. The language was flowing and beautiful, much like the language of

Nantielle, Itale's own homeland, and he listened on with interest despite not having a clue what they were saying. It was just a relief to be out of combat once more. He had come far from the man who had cowered beneath his father's abuse, saved by the vampire Cassius. No longer did he shrink from a fight. No longer was he made to feel small.

He knew what he was getting himself into when he offered to accompany Tantien north. The Misfits were well on their way to Lyvira to put a god back to sleep while they sought out a god of their own. The idea of it made Itale shudder. He hadn't known the Misfits all that long, but the burdens they shouldered were heavier than he ever hoped to bear. It seemed like they were well on the path.

"They're getting bolder." Arlaynia stepped up next to Itale, lips pressed in a thin line. Arlaynia was Tantien's boatswain, a tall and proud eldrasi who took her job very seriously. Itale had initially been intimidated by her, given her bold words and lack of sympathy towards lazy sailors, but the crew had grown on Itale. He'd never interacted much with eldrasi in the past, always too intimidated to approach any that had lined the shores of Nantielle with their ships. Still, he was coming to find them admirable in so many ways.

Tantien's hammer swung to his side as he nodded, peering out at the rough seas. Off in the distance, several heads of Delroy's hydra peeked above the surface of the water as she swam near the vampire pirate's ship. The dragon had never come near enough for Itale to be certain how many heads it had, but she was still beautiful to watch, her scales gleaming beside the trails of ice in the water. The ship she sailed with, the Crimson Nightshade, was as terrifying as she was beautiful, with torn black sails and cherry wood. The figurehead was nothing more than a bone-white skeletal structure that hugged the bow. Delroy flew his flag high, a skull with vampire fangs, and Tantien frowned as he raised his palm to his brow.

"Arlaynia, have Yír signal Delroy. It is high time we meet again. We're drawing close to dangerous waters."

Itale gave Tantien a sharp look. "These haven't been dangerous?"

The smile Tantien flashed was wild and tugged at something deep in Itale's belly.

"I'm afraid not."

The tendrils of magic were always pulled taut when vampires were aboard the Firebrand, tangled up and at war: the undeath of vampires versus the life of the eldrasi. Itale still didn't understand it much, but tension clung to his shoulders and draped over his skin like a cloak as

Delroy and a few of his sailors stepped off their ship and reappeared on the Firebrand.

"I knew you would be callin' upon me soon," Delroy said, flashing a fanged smile at Tantien. His locs were tied back beneath his massive hat, decorated with beaded bones that gleamed against the darkness of his hair. "Da seas be lashing out in anger, but it is a strange anger."

"I feel it, too," Tantien said. "It's as if we sit at the edge of a storm but we're not sure when it's going to come."

Itale shivered. The air that brushed against the nape of his neck beckoned the promise of something dark. Something that danced at the edges of the horizon.

"Der is a clusta of islands due north der," Delroy said, gesturing towards the lowering sun. "Just a day's travel. My men tell me der dat ghosts haunt da shores, but Vykra have been sailing der as well." His gaze darkened, the puckered decay of his cheeks particularly pronounced as he drew closer. Many of the eldrasi sailors kept their distance, except for Tantien, who stood tall and stubborn against the brush of death magic that permeated from Delroy and his crew. "I believe dey are close to finding what we also seek."

"The Vykra are not our concern. It is who they serve that we hunt," Tantien said. "Her and the weapon we can use to put her back to sleep. Or kill her. I don't care which."

Delroy studied him with a cool expression. "Yes. But dey might have information that could be useful to us. I know it isn't only the Phoenix Mother dat you seek, Tantien. Der are rumors dat Zulthraine is sailing da seas again. It is...ah...understandable if your priorities are elsewhere."

Tantien's demeanor sharpened and flipped, tensing from his easy-going nature. Still, a smile remained perched delicately on his face, his eyes blazing with some unknown anger as he stepped forward.

Itale suppressed another shiver. He'd never seen Tantien this way, even in the midst of battle.

Delroy shifted but stood tall as Tantien approached. The ship had gone deathly quiet and still, and Itale cleared his throat nervously as he thought of approaching. Fear stayed his hand. He still didn't know what Delroy and Tantien were both capable of. What could Itale possibly do to calm them?

"Regardless of what you think you might know, Delroy, you speak too plainly. I am just as concerned with finding Rhavna as you are."

"Of course. Just don't lose your head along da way, hm?" Delroy's red eyes gleamed as Tantien grew eerily still. Tension was palpable in the air as the anger melted from Tantien's face and his expression took on an easy manner once more.

"We'll make sail towards the islands you speak of. Perhaps we can secure more information on Rhavna's whereabouts." At Tantien's words, Delroy nodded and turned on his heel. Without another word, he burst into a flurry of screeching bats and took off back towards his ship.

The Firebrand was silent for a moment before Tantien snapped his fingers. "This ship won't sail itself. Yír," he called up to the myrlír. "Keep a watchful eye on the horizon. Northern waters breed hardier folk, and we eldrasi were not made for the cold."

Yír nodded down as Tantien edged towards the stairs that led up to the wheel. Itale's teeth chattered as the wind brushed mercilessly against his bare skin, and he reached out to stop Tantien, then thought better of it and let his hand drop to his side.

As Itale watched Tantien disappear up the stairs to the wheel, he couldn't help but wonder what dangers they were about to walk into.

FIVE
TANTIEN

Delroy's words still stitched anger into his lungs, his breathing ragged as Arlaynia approached with furrowed brows. She appeared concerned, but Tantien had little time to ponder over it as his fingers slipped over the wheel of his ship. He needed to keep himself busy. "Ensure the deck is washed vigilantly after the bloodshed. Have the sailors toss the dead overboard. I'm certain Delroy's hydra will enjoy the meal," he told Arlaynia, waving her away when her mouth opened to speak. "And Arlaynia? Please ensure the Vykra we captured is secure. I'll be paying him a visit soon."

He waited long until after she'd left to slump over, to allow the weight of his fears to crash back down on his shoulders. Delroy had stirred up long-buried insecurities that his home had instilled guilt in him. He recalled all of his times as a young boy, when he and his sister were so full of dreams to prove themselves and chase away the stain their grandfather's curse had left on their family.

"One day, you'll understand." He'd only met his grandfather once when he was a child, when the scorn of his people hadn't yet chased him from the shores of Míradan. His grandfather was an intimidating man with stronger beliefs, determined that he had done the right thing by stealing a seed from their god's tree and planting it on the island the eldrasi now called home.

Tantien was still waiting to understand. His people were scorned by their god, cursed with humanity because of his grandfather's greed. What more could there be to understand?

His fingers curled so tightly around the wheel that they ached. Igraine had given up trying to locate their grandfather, convinced he had died at sea. Still, something whispered inside Tantien, a soft demand to keep searching, that their grandfather yet lived. Only he knew of the curse in its entirety; only he knew how to break it.

"Ely," he barked, waving at a young eldrasi as he helped another sailor tip a corpse overboard. Ely was one of their newest recruits: his hair was a dirty blond and twisted into a loose bun with several metal earrings pressed into his ear. The curse had made Ely almost entirely human, save for the pointed tips of his ears and the dashing of moss that collected at his temples. He was one of the hardest workers Tantien had ever had the pleasure to hire.

As Ely approached, Tantien gestured to the wheel. "Take over. I'm going below decks if anyone should need me."

Ely nodded wordlessly. Tantien figured he'd only ever heard one or two words from the boy, as stoic as he was determined to work hard. Just the way Tantien liked it, if he were being honest with himself.

Swinging away from the wheel, Ely replaced him with ease, and he descended the steps. He hadn't much liked tea until he met Itale, but the man had quickly changed his mind on the matter the last time they'd traveled together. The trip to Lyvira, undertaken while the Misfits were in Míradan rescuing Rooster's crew from prison, was a massive waste of time. However, the friendship that blossomed between Tantien and Itale made the detour worthwhile. There had been no sight of his grandfather then, but perhaps it would be different this time.

"I think some tea and company would be wonderful if your invitation still stands..." Tantien trailed off as he stopped at Itale's door, noting the serious expression on Itale's face as he poured a small vial of something dark into his teacup. Itale jumped, a startled expression crossing his face, and some of whatever he was pouring into his tea got on his hand.

"I apologize," Tantien said as distress crossed Itale's face and he attempted to get the liquid into his tea. "Was that important?"

"Very," Itale muttered quietly. "It, ah—is difficult to obtain but something I need to live."

"Are you sick?" Tantien hovered near the door. He wasn't one for nerves, having spent his entire life with the ease of being desired, but there was a tickle of some unease at the base of his belly now, an uncertainty until Itale waved him in to sit across from him at his table. He had an entire tea set laid across the table, the tea cups made of fine porcelain that had been chipped from travel. It looked well-loved, though, and Itale quickly filled another cup with tea as he leaned back and shook his head.

"No, no. It's a potion I take to ensure I live the way I was meant to." Itale, however, was prone to nerves. Tantien had watched him closely for some time after growing fascinated with the knowledge that he was a necromancer, and he'd never witnessed someone so twitchy in their behavior. Save for maybe Rackjack, maybe. When Itale's eyes flickered to meet Tantien's, they were full of hesitation.

"I don't mean to pry—" Tantien said, holding his hand up. "You don't have to speak of it if you don't want to."

The curls of Itale's hair bounced with the slight shake of his head. "I'm trying to learn how to be brave. I've learned a lot about courage since traveling with the Misfits and being on this ship." He inhaled deeply and took a long sip from his teacup before he set it down, the cup clinking loudly against its saucer.

"I was born a woman and lived that way throughout my adolescence even though I always knew something was off." He glanced sideways at Tantien again, who blinked and opened his mouth to speak. Itale continued before he could say anything. "*Maudre*, erm...my mother, she welcomed me when I came to her with it. I think I was thirteen winters at the time. It was my father that scorned me. How lucky was I that my mother should die while my father remained." Itale's expression twisted. "The potion helps me. I take it once a month, preferably on a day of the full moon. It helps me." His laugh mirrored his nervousness. "That's all."

Tantien reached out to grab his tea cup and lean back in his chair, raising his leg to rest his ankle on his opposite knee. "Eldrasi and drikoty cultures are fluid when it comes to gender, you know. It is why Linda is able to be so unapolegetically *them*. Drikoty have three genders, and because of the nature of their reproduction, they get to choose when they're old enough to do so."

"I'm not familiar with their culture well enough. I didn't know."

Tantien nodded and swirled his tea before taking a tentative sip. Ah, not too hot and bitter, just as he liked it. Itale must have remembered to sweeten it with honey.

"It is believed that the dragons were little more than goo of starlight in the sky, and some of that goo fell down and grew in pools upon Vilanthris' earth. Krokida and greka are born from those pools. If you believe such things. It is what the greka teach their young, anyway.

"Eldrasi are more fluid. Some of us like myself are more rigid in their identity." His grin turned wolfish as he flashed it in Itale's direction. "I know who I am and what I like. Many eldrasi are the same, but they flow through their identity like the wind carries through the trees. It's quite beautiful."

"You speak highly of your people," Itale said, a sad smile crossing his face. "I'm sorry they scorn you."

"They are a good people," Tantien agreed. "Much kinder than humans are most of the time." His smile faltered. "Much less likely to forget and forgive, though."

Silence fell between them until Tantien gestured to the empty vial that now sat next to Itale's teacup. "Give me a list of what's in that potion. I'll ensure next time we're able, we have the ingredients on hand."

Itale's eyes flashed with surprise and some unknown expression as his gaze landed on the vial. "I'm not sure what's in it. I can write to the apothecary in Nantielle and have her send the list, though. I should have enough until we next make port."

Tantien gave a firm nod and an easy smile. "We'll make sure you don't run out."

Itale lowered his head, but not before Tantien caught a glimpse of a smile that twisted at his lips. "Thank you." He stilled as a tension filled the room, and when he met Tantien's gaze, there was uncertainty in his eyes, his mouth parting as no words left his lips for several moments.

"Who's Kindroth?"

Tantien stilled. The name rekindled the flame of anger in his belly, the twist of guilt and bitterness that soured his tongue. "That's the name of my family, but Delroy was speaking about my grandfather," he said quietly, noting how Itale's nostrils flared and his eyes widened.

"Now it's my turn to apologize for prying," he said, nearly knocking his teacup over in his attempt to raise his hand and wave it in protest.

Tension bled into the air once more. The entire reason Tantien had sought Itale out was to run from the complicated feelings his grandfather's name always brought to the surface, but now they burned through his veins and reached out with prickly fingers to squeeze his heart.

"Ever the curious," he said, forcing an easy smile. He couldn't hide the pain that colored his gaze, but perhaps Itale would be fooled by the simple shrug of his shoulder as he sighed and turned his head to stare out of the small, round window in Itale's room. Big chunks of ice sailed through the water as they passed, and Tantien suppressed the urge to shiver. They were officially in the North.

"If you don't want to talk about it—" Itale trailed off, clearing his throat awkwardly as Tantien pinned him to his seat with a stare. He wanted to talk about it as much as he tried to keep it locked away in the hollow of his ribcage, shackled by chains and years of suffering familial betrayal.

"Let us just enjoy the small victory we shared today. We lost only a few of my sailors and managed another evening of survival for this lovely tea." He raised his teacup and clinked it lightly with Itale's when he did the same, and the tension slowly seeped out of the room. He sensed Itale's curiosity sifting between them like a fog. Still, Tantien did not have the heart to speak on his family's curse and what it had cost them when his grandfather plucked a seed from their god's tree back in Daesthara. Too much. So much so that Tantien's soul cried out for salvation every day. He wouldn't stop until he found it. For himself. For Igraine. For their family line. No one else would suffer at the hands of that curse, not like his parents had.

"Tantien?" Itale's soft voice pried him from his spiral, and he smiled gratefully.

"Tell me Itale, what is your home like? I have not been to Nantielle save for the occasional port stop to resupply. What are the people like? The food? Tell me everything."

Itale's eyes lit up, and he nodded enthusiastically. As he began to speak, Tantien leaned back in his chair and raised his cup to his lips, allowing himself to drift away into Itale's vivid descriptions of pastries and the rich culture of his homeland.

SIX
ITALE

By the second week of sailing, Itale found himself growing miserable at being stuck at sea. The winds had not been favorable, quite the opposite, and a nasty storm had knocked them off course.

He wanted to like it. Tantien seemed right at home on his ship, as did his crew, but a pit remained simmering in Itale's belly, not ever quite accustomed to the dip of the waves. He couldn't decide where to spend his time—his room, where the waves seemed less extreme, or above deck, where the company of the sailors could keep him distracted.

"Come and sit, Itale." Yumai waved him over, and Itale complied gladly. Yumai was the first eldrasi to be so open and fluid with their gender, as Tantien had mentioned to him a couple of days ago. Itale had been overjoyed to spend so much time with Linda, who was still discovering who they were, but he was quickly growing fond of Yumai's company as well. The Misfits and Tantien's crew had shown Itale what it was like to be around those who accepted him and his identity. He'd spent so long isolated by his father's disgust, he thought that's how it was everywhere.

The Misfits had shown him a different path.

Sitting on a short crate next to Yumai, he smiled miserably. He wasn't suffering from seasickness anymore, not in the same way that Helai had when they'd boarded the ship to sail from Alavae to Míradan. Still, the heaviness sat in his belly all the same, and his headache was merciless. The day he got to set his feet on the ground, he'd surely kiss it.

"Have you heard, Itale?" Yír asked.

"Heard what?"

Yír glanced about, his cheeks bulging as he swallowed slowly and swirled the potion in his flask. "What we're really after here."

Itale hesitated. He didn't want to pry. A small part of him knew they were chasing more than just the Phoenix Mother. He also didn't want Tantien to think poorly of him if he were to find out his crew was talking about him behind his back. Despite it, he leaned in, driven by his insatiable curiosity and the beast within that compelled him to draw forward. He shook his head softly, and Yír grinned, his teeth stained from the health potion.

"Have you heard of the Kindroth curse?"

Itale shook his head.

"I don't know that we should be—"

"Quiet, Yumai. He deserves the right to know what he's getting into."

Ely sat still as stone as Yumai and Yír bickered, his eyes turned up towards the wheel, where Tantien was sailing the Firebrand himself. It didn't appear as if he heard their conversation, but Itale stared up at him nervously. He imagined the hurt on Tantien's face if he knew Yír spilled his secrets, and his stomach lurched in response.

"I actually don't think I need to hear this." Itale pushed himself to his feet. "If I hear the story at all, I want to hear it from Tantien. Whatever dangers we're about to sail into, I'll be ready." It couldn't be any worse than being at the party where Rhavna was resurrected, or fighting in a war between two countries. Whatever the Kindroth curse was, it couldn't be any worse than suffering at the hands of his father, who would never see him as anything other than a woman.

He found himself wandering the ship even though he'd done so many times already. There was something comforting about it, the way he reveled in the way the boat seemed alive. There were times when Itale felt like a walking corpse, a mirror of the death magic he wielded. The Firebrand chased away the overwhelming and numbing sensation of the magic pressing against him.

"You'll tell me where he is."

Tantien's voice wafted through an open door into a room at the back of the hull, behind a couple of cells for any prisoners the Firebrand might take. One of the cells was unlocked, its door slightly ajar, and Itale drew forward despite himself, his curiosity getting the better of him.

Whoever responded did so in a foreign language, their voice low and ragged. There was a squelching sound and then a grunt of pain. The sharp smell of copper permeated the air, and Itale hesitated before looking through. He didn't want to be caught, especially not by Tantien.

A grotesque sight met him. Tantien stood facing the door, his face pinched with rage. It burned in his expression, his hair a halo of red around his head as he lashed out and struck the person in the chair in front of him. It was the Vykra they'd taken captive.

The captured Vykra spat at Tantien, and it hit his cheek, surprising him. It startled Itale too, who flinched from the sight as his foot caught the frame of the door and he and Tantien's eyes met. Panic flourished through him as he stumbled away before he could explain himself. Was Tantien torturing that Vykra? Why? It was apparent that Tantien was looking for someone, but he hadn't worked out who it was. Not yet. Perhaps it was his grandfather, as Delroy had mentioned.

"Itale, I have need of your magical capabilities if you have a moment." Tantien appeared at the door, startling Itale, who shied towards the stairs.

"I—I don't know if..." Catching the desperation pinched in Tantien's features, Itale's resolve began to crumble.

"Please."

Itale hesitated, then nodded meekly and followed Tantien back into the room. The air was thick with the copper stench of blood, and Itale couldn't help but stare at the slumped-over Vykra in the chair. He knew immediately that he was dead. A dark thought festered at the back of his mind: *Good. He deserved it.* Did he, though? Itale did not know much about Volreyan culture, save for the constant war between them and the kingdom of Kreznov. Something had pushed the Vykra south from their wintery continent, and they had been encroaching on Kreznov territory for a long time before Itale was born. Up close, the Vykra were even more intimidating than Itale realized, even dead.

"Did you kill him?" A foolish question, as Itale had seen him alive just moments before, and he did not turn as he felt Tantien sidle up behind him.

"Yes. A bit too heavy-handed, I'm afraid. I couldn't get him to talk. I was hoping you could bring his spirit back to interrogate. They're a bit easier to question."

"Ah," Itale said, biting his lower lip. "I'm not sure I'll be able to… spirits are Cassius' thing, not me. I'm better with working with the flesh." Glancing up, Itale met the blazing inferno in Tantien's gaze. "I can try, though. The spirit should still be here since he hasn't been dead for very long."

Tantien nodded silently as Itale moved forward, his fingers reaching out to touch the Vykra's arm. Blood stained the man's face and chest from where he'd been beaten to death by Tantien, his eyes still open, bloodshot and piercing blue. It frightened Itale how unaffected he'd become surrounding the dead, and he shuddered as he reached out with his magic to seek the Vykra's spirit. Finding the presence of spirits had always come easily to Itale; it was how he had discovered his knack for necromancy in the first place, but flesh was easier to manipulate. Spirits were the pure essence of emotion, and the Vykra's spirit was made of pure, white-hot anger.

The moment Itale brushed against the spirit's presence, he hissed and recoiled as if he'd been burned. Sweat pooled at his hairline and dripped down his face. He grit his teeth as he lashed out again in an attempt to pluck the spirit and put it temporarily back into its lifeless body.

"Itale—"

"Give me a minute," Itale grunted as he exhaled sharply, only to yowl in pain as the spirit burned him again and tugged away. The spirit howled as it manifested in the air behind the Vykra, red and angry, and Itale glowered at it as the room was sapped of all its heat, leaving a bone-chilling cold in its wake. It was simply too strong, and Itale gasped as he released his hold on the spirit. It sailed over their heads and hit the window behind them, rattling the glass before everything went incredibly still.

"I'm sorry, I couldn't..." Itale's voice shook, and he winced as he pulled his hand from the Vykra's arm, where a handprint had been burned into his skin. Itale's hand ached, and he turned as Tantien gritted his teeth in frustration and fled the room, leaving Itale alone with the corpse. The silence was overwhelming, and Itale gripped his wrist as he quickly followed Tantien's lead and left the room.

Embarrassment colored his cheeks as he hurried back up to the deck of the ship, where the frigid air cooled his face. He tilted his chin up as he pressed his hands to the railing of the boat and shut his eyes, willing his heart to stop beating so quickly.

What was it that Helai told him to say when he was feeling overwhelmed?

Clear soul—no. Clear mind, clear soul. That's what it was.

He thought that to himself until the anxiety untied itself in his chest and he opened his eyes, staring up at the twinkling lights in the night sky. The sounds of the waves lulled him away from his panic, and he exhaled softly. Perhaps he should have been firmer and denied Tantien's request to try to bend the spirit to his will. The spirit's presence lingered in the underside of his skin, making him shiver as he watched Tantien pace the length of the deck, only to disappear into his forge with a slam of the door.

Itale's own anger peaked, waking from its slumber. He wasn't one to let anger fester, but he was tired of being the blind dog.

It was time to get some answers.

SEVEN
ITALE

"Tantien?" Itatle's knuckles pressed against the wood of the door.

The door slipped open, and Itale poked his head in with uncertainty staining his expression. All of his determination to get answers died at the door when he felt the tension bleeding into the air. The forge was dark, but the door to Tantien's bedroom was ajar, much like the room where he'd been torturing the Vykra. Itale approached, urging the door open.

"Unless you're here to drink with me... fuck off." The dark red silk of Tantien's hair was in a disarray around his sharp features as he bent his head forward, towering over the desk across from his bed. One hand curled around the lip of his desk, the other nursing a bottle, which he drank deeply from without bothering with a glass. A sharp scent infected the room, like the cross between smoke and ocean salt, and Itale steadied his nerves as he forced himself inside. He wouldn't be chased away by the bite of Tantien's words, and his eyes narrowed.

"Okay. Pour me a drink then."

Tantien raised his head, and the impossible blue of his eyes widened slightly in surprise as if he hadn't expected Itale to accept his offer. There were still flecks of blood on his fingers and the hollow of his cheeks as he moved over to a cabinet and pulled a glass out, pouring Itale a generous amount of Vitreusian rum—Carter's rum. Itale found himself wondering how the Misfits were doing, if they were safe. He worried about the other members of their group, fearing they faced many of the same dangers.

"Thank you," he said softly as Tantien offered him the glass.

Tantien waved a hand in response as he leaned against the desk and raised the bottle to his lips. The eldrasi kept his composure well for someone whose bottle was nearly empty.

Itale took a tentative sip, then grimaced. He much preferred his tea.

"You weren't meant to see that. I don't enjoy sharing that part of myself," Tantien admitted quietly, staring out at the angry sea as waves crashed against the side of the ship. "And I shouldn't have asked that of you. Sometimes I forget myself when it comes to something I want."

Itale blinked and hid himself behind his drink. "Did he tell you anything before he died, at least?" he asked finally.

Tantien shook his head after a long draw from his bottle, "No, though I believe he had the information I sought."

"What's so important? What information did that Vykra have?" The words left Itale's lips before he could decide if they should be spoken at all, and Tantien gave him a sharp look that had Itale sipping nervously at his drink. His eyes watered as the rum burned his throat, but he kept his gaze locked on Tantien, refusing to flinch away.

"I believe they know where my grandfather is. Something he said to me when we were fighting."

A chill stretched throughout the room, unnaturally so; it was like Itale's necromancy, only not. It was as if they touched the essence of trepidation, like the warmth of the flames in the torchlight was pried from the fire.

"I take it you're looking for him?" Itale found enough courage to take a step forward, to seek out the heat that always seemed to roll off of Tantien. Perhaps it was the fire in his veins, the very fire Itale often saw drenching his expression. He hadn't pried before when Tantien mentioned his grandfather, but he would now. He needed to know what he had signed up for on the shores of Vitreuse when he offered to accompany Tantien and his crew north.

Tantien nodded. Slowly. Solemnly. Then sighed.

"I believe killing him will set things right with my people. Will right the curse on my family's name. Will save my sister and I's souls from being devoured by Bulgash."

Itale felt giddy. He was finally getting the answers he craved, but was too polite to ask.

"Who's Bulgash?"

"One of the dragons. The one waking. The one the Misfits have gone to put back to sleep." Worry wracked Tantien's tone, his expression rugged, and Itale's heart plummeted anxiously to his stomach at the thought.

"Do you think you'll be able to?" Itale asked. "Kill your grandfather?" Itale didn't think he'd have the courage to kill his own father, even during times when his father was being...well, his father. The emotional scars that peppered Itale's soul from all of the harsh words his father had spoken could never drive Itale to seek such intent. Maybe he'd feel differently now if he saw him again.

"I've been preparing for the opportunity since I was a young man," Tantien said, his voice low with determination. "The eldrasi you see, those who dwell on Míradan? They all suffer from my grandfather's decision. He condemned them to a curse when he stole a seed from the God Tree in Daesthara. He sentenced them by stripping away the roots of who they are and making them almost like humans." He frowned, then smiled sheepishly at Itale's frown.

"Humans are not all bad. That was cruel."

Itale nodded. "It was. There are many of us that are good."

Tantien studied him silently. Itale didn't know where to look, his eyes darting about the room as they settled anywhere *but* Tantien.

"Like you?" A new energy infected the air as Tantien set his glass down, his gaze burning as Itale met them. He moved slowly around the desk as Itale became painfully aware of the tiny space between them. A nervous and excited thrill coursed through him as he raised his mug to his lips in an attempt to distract himself from such ner-vousness.

"Well yes. B-b-but I was also talking about people like Sígrun, Skin-ny Jim, Habal, Carter." He backed up, surprised when he thumped against the door of Tantien's bedroom. With nowhere to go, he watched Tantien approach, his mouth dry, his heart thundering in his ears. He gripped his mug so tightly his fingers ached. "There are plenty of good people in the world if you know where to look."

Tantien hummed in acknowledgment, but Itale could tell he wasn't thinking about the conversation anymore. If Itale was being honest with himself, he wasn't either. They had been through so much battle and uncertainty in the past week, it was nice to feel something other than fear. A slow heat crawled down and curled low in his belly, and Tantien pressed a flat hand against the door next to Itale's head as he leaned close.

It was almost painful how *alive* Tantien felt. Like a moth drawn to a flame, Itale couldn't help himself as his hand darted out to rest against Tantien's chest. His shirt had been ripped open at the top, and blood still flecked his skin from the vkyra he'd interrogated. It was the slow, steady thump of Tantien's heart beneath his fingertips that drew Itale in. He sensed death around them all the time. The yawning crawl of the void. It sapped the warmth from his body, took the life from the tips of his fingers. Somewhere on the ship, a small rat died from the wrath of Arlaynia as she collected a crate from the hull. Itale felt the moment the rat's tiny heart stopped beating, and was almost immediately swept away by the demanding presence of Tantien's. It was incredible.

"Gods, I want to—" Tantien's breath teased Itale's face as he tilted his head upward to meet Tantien's gaze. His hair was in a disarray, hanging loosely and chaotically about his face, and Itale was tempted to reach up and tuck it behind his ear. They shouldn't. They were ruled by distraction. This was nothing. And yet...

"What's that?" Itale whispered, almost afraid that speaking too loudly would break whatever was happening. Desire filled him so fiercely that he trembled as Tantien drew even closer, his lips inches from Itale's. His fingers darted through the soft tendrils of Tantien's hair, pushing it away from his face before he could lose his courage.

"I want to kiss you—"

The tension broke as the ship lurched, knocking Itale's head into Tantien's nose.

A low groan passed Tantien's lips as he backed up, nurturing his nose with his fingers.

"Oh gods, I'm so sorry." Itale reached forward as the ship lurched again, flinging him once more. Tantien caught him, his head turned up towards the ceiling, and he growled in frustration.

"What the *fuck* is happening out there?" As Tantien made sure he was steady on his feet, Itale had the embarrassment to blush, his eyes darting down as Tantien brushed past him to pull open the door. If he was intoxicated, he showed no signs of it as Itale followed. The forge beyond was quiet and dark, but distant shouting behind the door to the forge had both Itale and Tantien forgetting their moment as they both stumbled towards the deck of the ship.

Chaos met them.

Itale sensed Yumai's death as she dropped, their body carried overboard before Itale could process what had happened. A low cry escaped his lips, but Yumai was gone, swept away by the sea. It was dark, the blanket of night a shield for whatever enemy lay waste to their ship, and Itale gripped the railing as eldrasi began shouting in their native tongue. They did not care that Itale could not understand them, their panicked cries silenced as Arlaynia and Tantien barked orders and scrambled to their stations.

A shadow moved near one of the masts, a transparent thing that ripped itself from the wood. It yowled, a high-pitched scream that had Itale bending over with his hands pressed to his ears. More shadows joined as some*thing* crawled over the side of the ship onto the deck, its monstrous head deformed and full of sharp teeth. It resembled a wolf with webbed feet and four thin wings protruding from its back.

"Daemon," Tantien shouted. "Yír, signal the Crimson Nightshade. There are demons about!"

Another wolf demon slunk forward slowly, drooling from a parted maw as it locked eyes with Itale. It sported six eyes, three on each side of its head, and its ears were long and thin as they jutted straight back from its skull. Two, human-like arms protruded from its middle, and a soft whisper caressed Itale's ear. He didn't understand the words spoken, and shuddered when he realized it was the *wolf* speaking to him, uttering soft temptations. It sank into Itale's skin, filling him with a rage he had never felt before. He wanted to sink his teeth into the nearest eldrasi's skin, wanted to lash out with his magic and poison Tantien's heart. How satisfying would it be to watch the light flicker from his eyes? How intoxicating, to kill...

The murderous, angry thoughts coursed through him until he was blind with rage, until his fingers twitched and he felt the soft caress of death against his skin. The strings that tied life to his magic were pulled tight, and he instinctively cut one, noting with a bitter satisfaction when a nearby eldrasi's arm began to rot and decay. Her screams were warped and slowed down, and Itale didn't register her pain until everything became loud. Until the whispering and the anger vanished as quickly as they appeared.

"Wha—" his confusion turned to horror as the eldrasi in front of him whimpered, clutching her injured arm. "Did I do that?"

"Itale." Tantien's voice carried over from where he stood, his hammer caked in blood. The demon lay upon the deck of the ship, its brains spilled out of its head, and its tongue hanging out of its mouth. As Tantien locked eyes with Itale, he nodded. "Steel your mind. They will try to tempt you to do terrible things." He hurried over to the injured eldrasi, his fingers grazing over her wound as he murmured something quietly in eldrasian. A soft, green glow grew beneath Tantien's fingers, and when he pulled away, the wound was completely healed. Itale flinched from the raw energy of *life* that soaked the air, but a large part of him was impressed by how easily

Tantien wielded the healing magic. Tantien didn't wield his magic often, but when he did, it was something to be admired.

A loud shout echoed over the ship, and Itale's stomach plummeted as Yír wrangled with another demon. This one was tall and vaguely human-shaped, but Itale's mind couldn't seem to understand its form, always slipping between the cracks of comprehension. It had Yír's throat in its bone-thin fingers so tightly that Itale sensed the slowing of Yír's heart. Itale's stomach leapt to his throat as he reached out magically for the dead wolf demon, his fear willing away his concentration. He couldn't get a grasp; his guilt over hurting that eldrasi was overwhelming, and he ground his teeth together and lost all feeling in his left pinky finger as the wolf demon twitched and was dragged to its feet. Brain matter trickled down the side of its face, and Itale commanded it forward. It crashed into the other demon, gnashing its teeth and clamping down on the demon's arm, prompting it to release Yír.

Yír fell to the deck of the ship, gasping and clawing at his throat as the demon shuddered out of sight, only to reappear in front of Itale. The stench of death permeated off of it as it lashed out and wrapped its too-thin fingers around Itale's throat, dragging him up so that only the tips of his toes pressed against the deck of the ship.

Itale didn't even have time to react as fragmented visions popped into his mind. *A small island somewhere further north, the peaks of the mountains that edged one side were jagged and tall. A small gathering of Vykra, chanting lowly in their native tongue, the shadow of a dragon god darkening the wall of the cliff they stood before. A large, wicked dagger with a white opal in its hilt.*

The moment the dagger entered Itale's head, he knew it was utter certainty: that was the dagger they were looking for. That was what could kill Rhavna.

The demon dropped Itale as it howled and disappeared in a trail of dark smoke. Itale barely noticed the pain from falling on his knees as he gasped for air, his palms pressed to the wood as he struggled to untangle the flickering images he had just seen.

Demons poured over the ship, overwhelming it, and Itale despaired. Everywhere he looked were demons. More and more climbed out of the water, clinging to the side of the ship, grabbing at eldrasi...

He blinked, and all of the demons were gone. Tantien stood a few feet away, his eyes aflame with fire burning brightly in the palms of his hands. The confusion in his face mirrored Itale's, and he slowly let the flame disappear as normalcy returned, suddenly and all at once. It was almost too much, and Itale trembled as he realized he was no longer using his magic. He looked down to see that the rest of his pinky was black and slightly decayed. The numbness had gone, only to be replaced by a vague, tingling sensation. He had no idea if feeling would return. The tips of all of his fingers were already black and unfeeling from the last time he'd used too much magic. He'd have to be more careful next time. Cassius had warned him against using more magic than he had the strength for, and this was an excellent reminder.

"Everyone who remains on this ship, report to this deck. Arlaynia, make sure everyone is accounted for. Kalíra, I need you!" Tantien turned his head up towards the night sky as a gryphon soared above, his wings tucked neatly at his side as he descended, landing on the deck with ease. A soft purr-like trill echoed against his chipped beak as Tantien brushed his fingers against his feathers, and then he swung onto his back.

"I must go speak with Delroy. Arlaynia, the head count."

"Wait." Itale reached out as he turned to go. "I-I need to speak with Delroy too. I think one of those demons showed me something. I..." he hesitated, his eyes darting around to the other eldrasi. His heart cried out in sorrow for the loss of Yumai, not yet able to grieve. Fragmented visions of what the demon had shown him flashed across the forefront of his mind again, and Tantien nodded, holding his hand out.

"Take my hand."

Itale glanced up at Kalíra, but since he didn't seem opposed to Itale joining, he slipped his hand into Tantien's and let him drag him up behind him. The saddle was too small for two people. Still, Itale didn't have time to feel embarrassed about how close he was to Tantien before the eldrasi was whispering words of encouragement to Kalíra. The gryphon took off with a fierce flap of his wings.

Itale's stomach plummeted, and he wrapped his arms around Tantien's waist as he squeezed his thighs against the saddle so tightly they burned. He'd watched Cassius fly with his horse Fírnster enough times to think it easy. How wrong he'd been. He liked flying perhaps less than he enjoyed sailing.

Lucky for him, Kalíra flew quickly, and they were descending towards the Crimson Nightshade before too long. The vampire's ship was teeming with undeath, with skeletons working the sails as vampires moved about in their unillusioned forms. Delroy stood at the helm and approached only when Tantien and Itale slid off Kalíra's back and took off again.

"I think I know where we're supposed to go," Itale said, side-eyeing Tantien as he gave him a surprised stare. His mouth had been poised open to speak, but he shut it as Delroy looked between them and then settled his red stare on Itale.

"Speak den, boy," he rasped, his hands clasped together in front of him. "An' quickly. Demons have laid waste to dem waters. I am needed to ward da ship from their evil ways."

Nervousness drew the confidence from his lungs. "I-ah, I-I saw something. An island with a mountain range, only the mountains were extremely jagged and different in s-sizes." Itale's stutter was slight but prevalent enough for him to be painfully aware of it. "I-I know it was further north somewhere. Vykra gathered there, and they had a dagger with an opal in the hilt."

Delroy's nostrils flared, but he said nothing as Tantien brushed forward, the deep slant of his brow furrowed as he frowned. "Demons are deceitful. Can we trust it?"

Hurt flourished through Itale at what felt like an accusation, but he swallowed his anger. Tantien was right. What gave the vision such legitimacy? It could have shown him anything.

"It matches da description, an' we have no otha leads. It is worth checking into," Delroy said, his fangs gleaming as he parted his lips in contemplation. "It is strange, though. We faced no such attack and we did not see any demons board your ship."

Tantien's eyes flickered with some emotion Itale couldn't discern. Shock, perhaps? Anger? "What?"

"Our ship remained untouched."

"Well," Tantien gestured about the ship, "You are a ship full of the dead."

Delroy laughed. "Yes, perhaps dat deterred dem."

Tantien's expression turned serious. "If the vision was legitimate, do you know the island Itale speaks of?"

Delroy grew still. Stiller than anything living could accomplish, his hand poised at his chin in thought. Exhaustion tinged Itale's expression, a headache worming its way at his temples. He wanted his tea and his bed so desperately that it ached like a physical thing he could grasp.

"I know where ta go, but dem waters are dangerous, even for Sollatso."

"We knew this would be a dangerous venture when we left the shores of Vitreuse." Tantien sighed, running a hand through his hair. "And I, unfortunately, cannot go with you."

Headache forgotten, Itale turned to Tantien, shocked. "What do you mean, we're not going with him? That's why we're here."

Tantien refused to look at Itale, his jaw pulsing as he stared at Delroy, his silence all encompassing. A chill rolled down Itale's back.

"You were questioning da young lad's vision only to succumb to ya own? Tantien, I didn't take you ta be one of dem foolish types."

"If there's even the slightest of chances I can locate my grandfather, I have to go. The island is not far from the weapon's location. It will not be a long detour."

Itale was convinced Delroy's stare could strip skin away until the soul was bare, and he shivered at how intimidating it was. He turned back to Tantien, trying to study the lines of his face. All he saw was the bitter desire for revenge.

"M-maybe we stop and think about this. The Misfits are counting..." he trailed off when Tantien's angry expression turned to him. *Don't lose courage. I have a right to speak my mind.* "The Misfits are counting on us to find out all we can about Rhavna. If we lose what lead we have, well...that could lead to severe consequences for all of Vilanthris."

"Da boy is right," Delroy said. "We don't have time to let family matters get in da way."

Tantien stepped forward, his voice lowering as he threw his hand out in frustration. "I do not expect either of you to understand, but I'm going. I won't let the trail grow cold again."

"If Rhavna and the weapon that can kill her slip through our fingers, den it will not matter if where your grandfather is. You will not have me beg, but I urge you ta see reason," Delroy said.

Itale nodded. It was hard to believe he'd ever agree with the vampire, but there was a manic look in Tantien's eyes. It simmered quietly behind some semblance of control, but it was there all the same, a maelstrom in his gaze.

All of it went still as he smiled. "Of course. You're right, Delroy. How silly of me. Lead on, and we will continue to follow."

Delroy's eyes darted between them as a vampire trailed close, uttering something quietly to the vampire captain. He nodded and then swept a hand over his chest and bowed stiffly.

"We keep to the path. The island is but a day or two travel to da northeast." He gave one last withering stare at Tantien before he disappeared to speak with some members of his crew.

Tantien said nothing as he called Kalíra back down, and Itale didn't push him to speak. Not when he knew what he'd just had to sacrifice to pursue Rhavna and the weapon they sought.

EIGHT
TANTIEN

He spent the better part of the next two days snapping at anyone who came near and holing himself up in his room, where he could pore over old maps and drink rum in peace. Isolation had made a home in him, convinced that no one else understood. No one else *did* understand; no one other than his sister, and she was a world away. She'd moved on, but Tantien couldn't. He wouldn't. If he did, there would be no one left to break the Kindroth curse.

The night before they were to arrive at their destination, Tantien slipped into his forge after speaking with Arlaynia about his intentions. She wasn't happy about his departure, but he knew her better than anyone. She would command his crew in his absence and keep them safe.

The forge was quiet and dark, and Tantien moved to the opposite side, where Kalíra was sleeping in the hole at the edge of the ship. His breathing was steady, but he wasn't one to wake in Tantien's presence. He oftentimes worked the forge late into the night. It was the only thing that could distract him from the uncomfortable feeling that had built in his chest all these years from chasing a ghost. The Misfits had significantly benefited from it, thanks to the weapons and other artifacts he had forged for them.

"Time to wake up, old friend," Tantien whispered, securing his hammer to the loop at his waist. He eyed his shield, but it was way too large for travel with Kalíra. He trusted his fighting skills enough to go without them. "I know, I'm sorry." He ran his fingers through the feathers at Kalíra's neck as he chirped in annoyance, one eye opening to meet his gaze. Gryphons were given to specific guards in the Thorns who were deemed worthy enough to ride them, and Tantien had been one of the few his age to have been given one to raise and train. He was Tantien's oldest friend, and his heart squeezed painfully at the memories they had been through together.

Kalíra nudged his palm with his head and then shook his wings loosely at his side as he stood. Above all else, he knew he could count on his gryphon. He was such a beautiful creature, his feathers a deep red that deepened to black at the tips. His bottom half and tail bore the appearance of a jaguar, his large, amber eyes brimming with intelligence.

"We're only going to be gone for a day or two. No one will even notice, if I have my way." He was kidding himself, of course. He was the Firebrand's captain; his absence would be noticed the moment the sun came up.

"Where are you going?"

Tantien turned as Itale pushed himself into the forge, his eyes wide with surprise. "I-I'm sorry. I knew you were probably feeling bad about having to ignore the lead on your grandfather, so I...uh...came to keep you company..." he trailed off, his gaze flickering from the hammer at Tantien's belt to the saddle on Kalíra's back. The realization on Itale's face plucked at Tantien's guilt.

"I won't hear a lecture," he said as Itale opened his mouth to speak.

"They need you," Itale said, glancing behind him. "The world needs you, Tantien. This—this revenge warpath you're on is only going to bring you more pain."

"Don't speak to me about pain. I don't expect you to understand," Tantien said bitterly, turning back to Kalíra. "I won't listen to your insult, Itale. This is my ship and I have made my decision. I mean to return before the Firebrand even lands on the island we sail to."

Determination set on Itale's brow. "Then I'm coming with you."

Tantien moved to deny him, then thought better of it. Itale had proven himself to be a worthy company, his necromancy unlike anything Tantien had ever seen. It may be wise to bring him along. There was a deep part of him that desired his presence, so he nodded. *Selfish and foolish. He'll be nothing but a distraction.* Itale had done something no one else could: he had weeded his way into Tantien and burrowed mercilessly in his chest. Cassius was the only other who had come close, and Tantien had run from him, allowing his fear of distractions to push him away. *In another life.*

But this one, this life, it had Itale. Demanding little thing.

Once more, he found himself wanting to kiss him.

He ignored the voice at the back of his head and smiled, a wicked grin as he gestured to Kalíra. "Fine, but we're taking Kalíra. Would you rather ride in front or back?" Satisfaction coursed through him at the flush of Itale's cheeks, his gaze flickering from Kalíra's saddle to Tantien.

"Front. I, ah, didn't particularly do well the last time we flew. Perhaps seeing where we are going will be better for me."

Tantien nodded, slipping a foot into one of the stirrups and swinging his leg over Kalíra's back. Flying with the gryphon was like second nature to him, but he recalled how nervous he'd been when he had ridden upon Kalíra's back for the first time. It had been without a saddle, as was custom to prove his worth to the creature. Their bond had been unwavering ever since.

He held out his hand to Itale, who avoided Tantien's eye contact as he swung up into the saddle. Itale sat stiffly in front of him as Tantien clicked his tongue and urged Kalíra from his hole in the wall.

"I'll have you know I'm still not happy this is happening," Itale uttered as the wind threatened to carry his words away. "This is a terrible idea."

"Good thing I didn't ask for your opinion on such matters," Tantien said, uncertain if Itale heard him at all as the wind yowled. Kalíra called out into the night as he spread his wings and took off, sailing high over the water as they flew east. It was a clear night, thankfully so, but the air was frigid this far north. Even with the furs they'd stolen from some of the Vykra they'd killed, they failed to chase the cold away, and Tantien's joints ached mercilessly. Eldrasi were not made for the cold.

The wind made conversation impossible, which Tantien was grateful for. The last thing he wanted to hear was Itale chastising him for abandoning Delroy and his crew. The image the demon had shown him burned into his brain, a vision that Tantien did not want to be true. His grandfather was an evil man, but Tantien had to believe he would not stoop so low as to work with demons.

And yet, the vision had shown him doing just that.

"Faster, Kalíra," he whispered in eldrasian, knowing, somehow, that the gryphon would be able to hear him.

And so he did. They took off quickly into the night, and Tantien's eyes were set upon the distant splattering of islands that touched the horizon. Itale's human eyes wouldn't have been able to see them, not with the blanket of night, but Tantien could. They would be there in a matter of hours, just before the sun woke.

Itale sat between his thighs, pressed rigidly against him as he clung to the saddle horn. His curls were a wild mess and prone to whipping Tantien in the face. It was an otherwise uneventful flight, and they made it to the island with no trouble.

The sea met the dark stone of the island's cliffside as Itale and Tantien slid off Kalíra's back, their feet landing heavily on the sand. Itale stumbled slightly but held his hand up as Tantien reached out to steady him, his mouth pressed as he glared.

Still wasn't happy with Tantien. Got it.

Several sea birds settled on the beach nearby, their soft chirps keeping the silence at bay as they trudged up towards the treeline. Kalíra ruffled his feathers as he took off, and Tantien's heart thundered in nervous excitement. His grandfather was close.

He had to be.

Prying his hammer from his waist, he twirled it as he contemplated. They couldn't search the entire island; it would take far too long. The forest here was dense, full of looming trees that bled with trepidation. Something begged him not to step inside, lest he get swallowed by its darkness.

"I sense something foul, something dead," Itale whispered, the anger drawn from his face. Fear replaced it, and he glanced up at Tantien as the eldrasi turned and locked eyes with the necromancer. "It's accompanied with something else, but I can't place what it is…"

A twig snapped nearby, and Tantien's eyes shot to the treeline, where some leaves rustled and then stilled. The wind, perhaps. Tantien knew better than to lower his guard, though. Especially this far north.

"Can you follow it?" Tantien asked, turning back to Itale. The boy's eyes were wide, so much so that Tantien could see them even in the blanket of night, and after a moment, Itale nodded, straightening.

"I think so."

Tantien nearly shivered from the anticipation as they both took their first step into the forest, and Tantien beckoned fire into his palm for a light source. He didn't use his pyromancy a lot—the fire magic was more suited to his sister's personality, but certain times called for it.

They'd have to tread carefully; there were likely Vykra about, and if his grandfather truly was on the island, his men would be here too.

The woods were still, so still that Tantien barely sensed the soft patter of the tree's heartbeats with his magic. Eldrasi were rooted to all life on Vilanthris, but trees especially so. The trees were their ancestors, from which the eldrasi were born.

"This way," Itale whispered, pushing through the brush and disappearing deeper into the forest. They were too far north for any bugs to survive the frigid temperatures, but Tantien knew that ice bears and wolves loved to inhabit these lands. There were rumors even of massive deer that dwelt on the islands, so he took care to walk quietly and keep his voice low.

They walked for most of the day in silence. Tantien sensed Itale's continued displeasure with him, and he thought it best not to push him. Not when Itale had come anyway. Not when Tantien was so close to his goals.

"I know you are displeased with my choice, but I am glad you are with me," Tantien finally whispered as Itale paused, his head cocked as if he were listening for something. Tantien was confident in his ability to fight and survive, should he need to, but he knew he was walking into a den of vipers. Having Itale and his necromancy would be invaluable.

"Someone has to keep you from getting yourself killed," Itale muttered, then stilled, glancing sheepishly behind him. "I-I mean... no, no. I meant what I said."

Tantien scoffed, laughter tinting the edges of his throat, and shook his head. Itale was right, but he wouldn't have had the courage to be so truthful just weeks ago. The Firebrand and her crew were rubbing off on him, it seemed.

"I don't know how I managed to survive so long without your protection," Tantien teased, stilling as another twig snapped somewhere off in the distance. His fire was smothered as he reached out and grabbed Itale by the back of the shirt, dragging him behind a tree. He ignored Itale's quiet protests as his arms encircled Itale and he drew close.

Itale's breathing was hot against his chest, the cold that radiated off Itale's skin seeping through Tantien's shirt as he leaned around Itale and the tree to peer out into the woods. A low clicking sounded in the treeline, followed by the sigh of a whisper, and then there was nothing but silence. There was so much trepidation in the air it tightened in Tantien's chest, but then it was gone, all at once. The woods returned to normal, the tension shattering like glass, and the soft cry of a bird broke the silence.

Tantien's shoulders sagged, and he peered down at Itale, whose chin was raised to meet Tantien's stare. Tension formed again, a new kind, the kind that had formed when he'd been drunk in his room and had Itale trapped against his door.

Itale's lips were parted, his eyes bright with some emotion. His cheeks were rosy from the cold, highlighted as the sun began to rise, and once more, an ache sang through Tantien.

He wanted desperately to kiss Itale. He wanted it so desperately it *hurt*, a great ache deep in his chest.

"Tantien..." Itale breathed, his fingers curling against the fabric of Tantien's shirt at his waist. "Get down."

A soft giggle tinkled against the wind as Itale jerked Tantien roughly to the side at the exact moment something shot past his left ear and embedded into the trunk where Itale just was moments before.

A low clicking mingled with song echoed through the forest as it rustled to life, and several beings stepped out from behind trees. Tantien stilled at their wild, untamed hair, blackened fingers, and deer masks, knowing immediately what they were up against.

"What is it?" Itale asked, noting Tantien's horrified expression.

"Witches."

NINE
TANTIEN

Tantien ducked past two more daggers that sailed over his head, his fingers reaching out to keep Itale low with him. He loathed witches. They worked with wild magic, magic untamed by any set of rules and guided by the dragon gods they worshiped. They were children of the forest, but they had turned their backs on their creators long ago to worship Motaumr, the dragon slumbering at the world's center.

"We are no match for them, Itale. We need to run," Tantien urged, his fingers curling around the hilt of his hammer. The witches moved around them on creaky limbs, flickering as they darted in and out of existence. One's mask was cracked, revealing the blackened rot of her teeth when she smiled, and she tilted her side as she darted forward. Tantien raised his hammer to strike out at her, and she flinched away, cackling.

"Go," he urged.

"I won't leave you," Itale protested, his face drawn in offense.

Tantien gritted his teeth in frustration as he shot forward, but they always stayed just out of range of his swings. He resorted to his pyromancy, but the fire never reached its target, snuffed out by the wild magic the witches wielded. He was never as good with his fire, not like his sister.

A fox, long dead and naught but bone, rose from the ground, its teeth clacking together as dark magic trailed from its spine. Itale's hand reached out to direct it as it lunged at a witch's legs, exploding on impact.

"I need one of them," Itale said. Sweat gleamed from his upper brow, his breathing shallow. There were maybe six witches in total, but it was difficult to discern for certain due to how often they disappeared only to reappear in an entirely new location. "If we can kill one—"

"Working on it." Tantien swung his hammer, satisfied when it made contact with a witch's head. Her mask shattered and fell to the ground, and she howled in pain and rage. Yellow-green sappy blood trailed down the side of her dirty face, her hair ratty and covered in twigs, and then she snarled; half of her teeth were missing.

"Fool," she rasped, her face flickering from monster to a woman of beauty with young, unblemished skin and piercing blue eyes. He found himself rooted in place; struggling as he did, he could not move, captivated by just how impossible the blue of her eyes was. Laughter echoed, high-pitched one moment, low and dark the next, as the bleeding witch trudged closer. Her face had settled into the illusion of a beautiful one, her mouth parted sensually as she reached out to drag a delicate finger down the side of Tantien's face. Her touch tingled with magic, and it wrapped around him, his mind growing hazy. Where was he? Who was this beautiful woman in front of him?

"Do you want to fuck me, Tantien? Do you find this visage desirable? Do you want to use me and throw me away like you do all of the others? Like you will him?"

He did not know how the witch knew his name as her hand moved to trail down his side to wrap around his cock through his pants. He moaned, simultaneously repulsed and seduced by her touch. He wasn't sure why.

Leaning close, the witch pressed soft lips to Tantien's ear. "Your grandfather isn't here. He promised to find you when he was ready for a family reunion, but wanted me to deliver a message." Her teeth dragged along his lobe as she slipped her hand into his pants and began to touch him.

"If you don't stop looking for him, he'll send someone to kill Igraine."

The illusion broke.

Fear and anger rolled over Tantien like a wave, and he attempted to pull away as the witch's spell broke. She didn't let him, her free hand curling possessively around the nape of his neck and dragging him close to slip her tongue into his mouth. Her kiss was foul, her strength rooting him in place, and Tantien's hand reached up to snake through her hair, to tug her back, to get her away…

He gasped as the witch disappeared, and he was liberated from her seductions. He dropped to his knees, scrambling for his hammer that had somehow found itself a few feet away on the ground. It was a comfort to have it in his hands as he shot around, but there were no more witches. It was as if they had never been there at all. Lightness returned to the air about the trees, the soft rustling of wind through the branches chasing away any lingering darkness. Sun filtered through the canopy, and Tantien's stomach rolled with disgust over what had just transpired as he knelt on his hands and knees and vomited.

Do you want to use me and throw me away? Her question echoed in his head, a mantra that tortured him as he shivered, his skin crawling from the ghost of her touch.

Your grandfather isn't here. Her words echoed through the trees like a mocking whisper, and tears pricked the corners of Tantien's eyes as he forced himself back on his knees in a sitting position and pressed his hands to his ears.

His grandfather wasn't here. Witches, like much of the ancient folk that originated from Daesthara, couldn't lie. The only reason Tantien was able to do so was because the curse his grandfather put on the eldrasi of Míradan had liberated them from the constraints of their roots.

If his grandfather wasn't here, that meant he'd made a grave mistake, that he'd allowed his mind to be swayed by the temptations of a demon.

"Itale, I—" he looked around, noting for the first time that Itale hadn't spoken since he'd called out for Tantien's aid. Terror flourished through him as he pushed himself to his feet and searched nearby. Perhaps he'd hidden. Tantien wouldn't have blamed him. "Itale, they're gone. Itale?"

He searched for several minutes to no avail. Angry clouds formed overhead.

"Itale," Tantien cried out, his panic swelling in his chest. "Itale!" He yelled until his breath was ragged as he ran through the forest, but it didn't matter.

Itale had disappeared.

TEN
ITALE

Laughter etched the air around him as Itale lashed out, seeking anything dead he could use to his aid. The corpses of the forest were aplenty, but it was spirits that came calling, beckoned forth by his call.

He was so focused on channeling the spirits that he didn't see her coming, his eyes rolled in the back of his head as his fingers plucked the strings tied to the dead.

He grunted, disoriented by the number of spirits that had trailed through him to borrow his strength. He'd killed three witches that way, the spirits screeching as they clawed at their arms and sank into their skin, forced them to slam their heads against rocks or gouge their own eyes out or slit their own throats. It was incredible to watch, but Itale had grown distracted when a witch pressed herself up against Tantien, who seemed both aroused and fearful of her. She was loathsome, more rotten than woman, with clumps of hair hanging loosely from her head and decay peppering her arms as flakes of skin trailed off and caught the sun's rays.

"Tantien." His voice was little more than a whisper, his strength ebbing as he directed the angry spirits of the forest towards the witch. "Go and help Tantien."

His command barely made it past his lips before something tackled him, and he hit the ground hard, a cry of pain liberating itself from his mouth as he landed sharply on his elbow. A witch clawed at his skin as she clacked her teeth together, her eyes wild with madness as she slipped her hands around Itale's throat and squeezed.

Itale struggled, his fingers curling through leaves and dirt, desperate for a rock or a twig or *something* to strike her with. He found nothing. Darkness peppered the edges of his eyes. He was drowning, drowning beneath the lack of air and the weight of the knowledge that he was going to die. Death didn't scare him. It hadn't even before he'd made it a second home in his skin, but he was still sad. Sad at the thought of leaving so many people he'd grown to care about behind. Sad that he would never get to say goodbye to Cassius and the other Misfits, the only family he'd known since his mother died. Sad that he would never get to hear Tantien laugh one last time. Sad that he'd never share tea with the other sailors on the Firebrand.

Suddenly, the fingers around his neck lessened, and he was gasping and curling over on his side as the dots popped into his vision, as glorious air drew into his lungs. It hurt to breathe, like he dragged his throat through glass shards, and tears pricked the corners of his eyes as something wet and metallic-smelling splashed across his face. Everything was blurry. His ears rang, a high-pitched echoing that made Itale want to cry out in frustration. His vision returned suddenly and all at once as a beacon of light lit up the forest.

Tantien.

It was Tantien, ablaze, fire licking his skin but not burning him, as his eyes turned gold with rage. He had the witch that had been trying to kill Itale tightly within his grasp, and she screamed and clawed at his arms as she began to burn.

"Don't you *dare* touch him." Tantien lifted her as her screams became high-pitched and her strikes against his arm grew feeble. Soon, she was nothing more than a charred corpse that Tantien dropped to the ground before making his way towards Itale. The fire that had once consumed him slipped away in the wind as he reached out for Itale.

Itale might have sobbed, had he had the will or ability to do so. Instead, he tucked himself into Tantien's offered arms, allowed the eldrasi's large form to envelop him as he pulled him into the shadow of a tree, where they both collapsed in each other's arms.

"You're okay. I've got you. I've got you." Tantien's words whispered into Itale's curls like a promise, and Itale allowed himself a moment to let go, to let the brushes of death wash away.

"Thank you," he rasped after several moments of gathering his bearings. He trembled against the warmth of Tantien's skin, trembled at the realization he'd almost lost his life. If Tantien hadn't been there...

"They will not touch you again, *daumïr*." The nantiellian word for 'soul of mine' made Itale's head raise, his gaze meeting Tantien's as he brushed the curls from Itale's eyes. He didn't know Tantien even knew his mother's tongue, but the way it rolled off the eldrasi's mouth made Itale shiver. There was also something strange burning in Tantien's expression, a blinding fire of determination that lit a flame of his own in Itale's chest. "I protect what is *mine*."

Tantien's confession sent the fire flourishing through him, and Itale reached a hand up, curled it around the nape of Tantien's neck, and crashed his lips to his. It felt like his soul screamed out. *Finally.*

Kissing Tantien shook the fear away as Tantien dragged him closer, his fingers clinging to Itale's waist in a demanding manner. Itale couldn't get close enough, his chest pressed against Tantien's, his fingers weaving through Tantien's hair. It was a fight against desperation as Tantien's tongue slipped past the barriers of Itale's lips, as it claimed his mouth and carried a soft moan from his throat. The dance around each other had grown agonizing, and Itale's disappointment was immense when Tantien pulled away, despite the ragged rattling in his lungs. He had nearly forgotten his close call with death as Tantien pressed his forehead against his, as his fingers reached up to brush delicately against his cheek.

"We need to return to the Firebrand," he said gently.

"We came here to find your grandfather," Itale protested weakly. His head spun, his stomach lurching with sudden nausea. His struggle to focus on Tantien was lessened as he turned to the side, afraid he was going to vomit. There were no dead witches around them, no spirits whispering softly in the air. All evidence of their fight had gone, as if it hadn't happened at all. It was like the demons on the Firebrand all over again; it made Itale feel like he was going mad.

"He's not here, *daumïr*." Tantien pulled Itale's curls from his face, but the feeling of nausea faded as Itale groaned, his fingers drawing to his throat. His skin was sore to the touch, and every time he swallowed, it was as if shards of glass had nestled there, content with injuring him every time he inhaled. "It appears as if we have been deceived. I—" Tantien's hesitation took his expression out towards the sea and the waves that crashed against the shore. "*I* have been deceived. I worry for Delroy. We must sail to him immediately. My grandfather will have to wait."

Itale's heart plummeted for Tantien. He knew the choke hold revenge could have on someone, knew how disappointed he must be to find the island empty of his grandfather. A gentle rain began to fall, and Itale tilted his head upwards, letting the droplets hit his face and aching throat. He didn't want to leave the warmth of Tantien's lap. Still, he knew that if they were deceived, there was a very real possibility that Delroy was in danger, that the Firebrand was in danger.

"The witches, they—"

"They're gone. I don't know what happened," Tantien said.

"But you saw them. We-we fought them?"

Tantien nodded slowly. "It is strange that they're this far north. There are stories of some of them settling in Kreznov, but to be on the islands of the north..." he trailed off and gave his head a slight shake. "No matter."

Despite everything, Itale could see the worry in Tantien's eyes, and it latched onto his own. If Tantien was worried, Itale knew he had every right to be too.

"Can you stand?" Tantien asked as Itale attempted to scoot off his lap. His voice was low and husky, and Itale had the embarrassment to blush as he met the molten gaze of Tantien's expression, as it burned away the anxiety in the eldrasi's eyes.

"Sorry," he whispered softly, pushing hurriedly to his feet. He still felt slightly unsteady, but he managed to stand, his fingers trembling. A headache was beginning to form at his temples and pinched at the bridge of his nose. He pressed his fingers to his head as he turned back towards the direction of the beach. His cheeks burned again as he recalled kissing Tantien, his heart thundering. He'd do anything to have that moment back, but reality had begun to set in. He straightened his back and swallowed his burning desires as he felt Tantien approach behind him and forced himself forward until they reached the edge of the forest. Angry clouds darkened the sky overhead, and waves crashed against the shore with reckless abandon.

"The sea has grown rougher than I thought. We may need to find shelter until the storm passes."

Tantien's words seemed to spur on the storm's wrath as the wind tore at Itale's hair and sand flecked up to hit at his ankles. There was no way Kalíra could fly with them in this weather, not safely.

"Come," Tantien said, turning deeper into the island. "Surely there is a cave we can shelter in. I may have seen one before we came across the witches."

They found a small pocket of caves just as the rain began to pour down. Itale was outright miserable, longing for the comfort of his room and his tea as he shook his hair from his eyes and let Tantien move ahead of him. The last thing they needed was to intrude on a bear's home. Especially on an island this far north. Itale had heard rumors of the size of beasts in the north, and didn't care to find out if they were true.

"I think everything is too wet to get a fire going," Tantien said, his voice tinged with apology as Itale's teeth began to chatter. His fingers had long since gone numb, and even the furs they'd stolen off the bodies of the Vykra were soaked through and did little to preserve the warmth radiating from his body. "But it appears as if this cave is unoccupied. We'll be safe here tonight." He spared a glance in Itale's direction and shook his head, disappearing out into the woods and returning not much later with a bundle of wet logs and sticks in his arms.

"I thought it was too wet," Itale said.

Tantien winked and dropped the logs near the front of the cave, far enough in that the rain couldn't touch them, but close enough they would fill their temporary shelter with smoke. They were lucky; the cave didn't seem to go too far in. If Tantien could get a fire going, it wouldn't take long to fill the space with heat.

"You are cold, and it's worth the attempt."

"I'm sorry you weren't able to find your grandfather." Itale almost didn't say anything, too nervous about upsetting Tantien, but something pulled the words from his chest, and Tantien stilled for a moment as he knelt over the pile of logs, and his shoulders sagged.

"He's been evading me for years. It doesn't come as a surprise that it wasn't any different this time."

Before Itale could answer, Tantien's back straightened, and he peered over his shoulder to smile at Itale. "No matter. One day I'll catch up to him and he'll get what he deserves." He waved a hand. "Please, Itale. Rest. You've been through a lot today."

You have too, Itale thought, but he did as Tantien asked. Exhaustion came for him quicker than he realized. Besides almost dying, they had trekked through much of this forest. They had fought many demons in the last several days, and the lack of sleep was finally beginning to catch up to him. As he slumped down against the wall of the cave, he found it difficult to keep his eyes open. It took Tantien little time to get the fire going, but he did, just as he promised, and his satisfied smile was the last thing Itale saw before sleep came for him.

ELEVEN
ITALE

The nightmare was subtle at first.

He stood upon a field, a lovely field of wildflowers and flowing grass. He couldn't recognize where he was... Rovania, perhaps, with its farmlands and wineries. The wind was just strong enough to pull at his curls, and Itale tilted his head back with his eyes shut, reveling in the sun's warmth.

Raise them.

A voice, soft as velvet, echoed through the halls of Itale's mind.

He opened his eyes and peered around, but noted nothing out of the ordinary. No, he wasn't in Rovania, he decided. He was in the countryside of Nantielle, where the sweet scent of honey bread passed through the air. Perhaps he could hunt down the source of that smell. He used to beg his mother to make him some of her famous honey bread.

Raise them.

There it was again. A stone of dread weighed down his belly as Itale spun around, seeing nothing but green as far as the eye could see.

But then he blinked.

The entire landscape changed, darkened by angry clouds overhead that threatened to spill rain. The grass was stained with bloodshed and gore as hundreds of people lay strewn about, their soft cries begging for liberation from their failing bodies. Many were already dead.

Tears of horror rolled down Itale's cheeks. He tried to move, but he was rooted in place, unable to comprehend the sight before him. Many of them were humans from the eastern continent, but there were Vykra, dwarves, and rakken too. A strangled sob curled around Itale's throat as he sought out the dead faces of his friends: Cassius, Rooster, Helai, Linda, Intoh, Rackjack: all dead, their stares long since glossed over and faded.

A woman appeared through a haze of fog, fabricated by the massive head of a dragon breathing steam from its nose. Her hair was like that of fire, with war paint etched across her face as she drew closer, her gaze turned down to the corpses of the Misfits.

"You can't save them. This is doomed to be their fate. They're just puppets, play things to meet an end. He is coming." The woman gestured up to the dragon, her smile of adoration bordering on manic. "And when he does, the world will be bathed in the salvation of fire."

Itale squeezed his eyes shut.

Wake up. Wakeupwakeupwakeup—

"Itale." Where Tantien's voice was gentle, his hands shook Itale roughly as he woke, a mixture of a scream and a sob tearing from his injured throat. Tears pricked the corners of his eyes as he curled in on himself, the echoes of the woman's warning still ringing in his ears.

"Get away from me," he cried, the shackles on his magic breaking as the shadows melted and forged wispy fingers that clawed at Tantien's hair and pierced his skin, drawing blood. Tantien hissed in pain and flinched away as Itale scrambled to his feet, still blinded by his recent nightmare.

He stumbled until his back was pressed against the opposite wall. His chest heaved, and only after several moments of wakefulness did the ghosts of his nightmare begin to fade. His magic retreated, and

Tantien remained sitting several feet away, his arms and shoulders weeping sap-blood.

"I hurt you," Itale whispered, horrified. "Oh gods…I've pushed my magic too far…" He collapsed, his arms encircling his waist as tears slipped down his cheeks. "I failed to help you, and now I've hurt you. I didn't even know I could call forth the spirits right now. I—" *Failure. Weak. Pathetic.* His father's words echoed through him as he cried. Distantly, he sensed a shifting of movement. Then Tantien was kneeling beside him, a curtain of red hair slipping over one shoulder.

"Come here."

Tantien left no room for resistance as he dragged Itale into his lap and pulled him against his chest. He was immediately enveloped in warmth and some earthy scent he couldn't place, and he nuzzled against Tantien until the claws of his nightmare had receded.

"You have nothing to apologize for," Tantien said, his voice rumbling against Itale's cheek. "We are not ourselves when the darkness of nightmares takes hold. Besides—" he laughed, a motion that shook both of them. "It would take a lot more than that to hurt me, *daumïr.*"

Silence enveloped them for a moment as Tantien spoke softly of his younger days, when he had served as a blacksmith for the Thorns, the guardsmen of Míradan. "Igraine had dreams of being a Thorn since she could speak, so when the opportunity finally presented itself to her, I knew I had to do what I could to keep a watchful eye on her. Ever the reckless my sister is," Tantien said, a soft, exasperated sigh pressing against Itale's hair. "I could never keep her out of trouble."

"Did she pull you into piracy then?"

Tantien's laughter was louder then, and it brought a smile to Itale's face. What a beautiful sound. How sweet it would be to be able to bottle it up and save it for rainy days.

"No, no. That was entirely my fault, but she embraced it way quicker than I did. I, ah…my obsession with locating my grandfather forced us to do some less than legal things and…well." He went silent after that, and a growing tension nestled between them. Itale became painfully aware how close they were and how warm it was as he raised his head to meet Tantien's waiting gaze.

"Feel better?" His voice was low, his mouth parted slightly, and Itale swallowed thickly as his eyes flickered from Tantien's mouth to his eyes and nodded. A violent chill coursed through him, the death and decaying of the island picking at his skin as he shivered from the cold. His fingers were numb, but he was *safe*. Safe and free from that woman. Safe and free in Tantien's arms.

"I do not want to go back to sleep," Itale confessed, fearful the nightmares would return. The fire was still blazing comfortably near the mouth of the cave, the roar of the storm outside echoing through the stone. For the first time since his magic manifested, Itale found himself fearing the darkness surrounding them.

Tantien's eyes darkened. "I can help with that." His lips lowered to press to the curve of Itale's jaw, his breath whispering against Itale's skin. "If you want me to stop, just say the word."

But Itale didn't. He didn't want Tantien to stop. His heart thundered in his ears, his stomach ablaze with desire as he tilted his head and granted Tantien better access to his neck. Tantien's lips were intoxicating, a flurry of warmth every time they pressed against his skin. This time, when Itale shivered, it wasn't from the cold. His core pulsed, knotted with desire, and a soft whine carved itself into the hollow of his cheeks.

"Tell me what you want, *daumïr*." Tantien's command was accompanied by the force of the storm, the thunder outside echoing throughout the mouth of the cave. Itale moaned, shifting on Tantien's lap and reveling in the growing erection that pressed against him from below.

"I want you," Itale whimpered, his cheeks flushed, his eyes bright. "Gods, I want you." He wanted Tantien more than he ever wanted anything or anyone in his entire life. It had struck him suddenly and out of nowhere, but now that they were here and Tantien was asking him what he wanted while he pressed small, sucking kisses down his neck, it was almost too much to bear. He ached so badly between his legs that he found himself tugging at Tantien's shirt. "I want this off."

Tantien complied immediately as Itale scooted back, pulling a low growly moan from Tantien's clenched teeth as his ass teased Tantien's cock. Satisfaction sang through Itale at how undone Tantien seemed to have become as he pulled his shirt up and off, and his stomach clenched mercilessly at the molten stare Tantien gave him. The eldrasi was beautiful, with broad shoulders and muscles that rippled with every movement.

"Lay on your back," he demanded.

"Why?" The question slipped past Itale's lips as he did what he was told, pushing himself off Tantien. The floor of the cave was cool, but the shiver that coursed through Itale was of anticipation as he lay down on his back.

"I've spent quite a long time wondering what ways I could make you scream. What ways I could make you say my name. What ways I could fuck you."

Itale lay his head back, trembling in anticipation as Tantien's form enveloped him, his eyes burning in the light of the fire. How Itale had gotten so lucky as to garner the attention of someone so beautiful, he wasn't sure.

"Too long. Do you know how beautiful you are? How fascinating? How strong? Gods..." he moaned, a soft, pretty noise that had Itale closing his eyes to liberate himself from the intensity in Tantien's gaze as he lowered his head to kiss Itale. He tasted of something sweet and rainwater, and Itale reached up to run his hands along Tantien's back as the eldrasi slowly worked on undressing Itale.

He tensed as Tantien worked to remove his pants, and Tantien paused, his head raising from where it was pressing a searing kiss to his hip to offer Itale a questioning stare.

"Sorry, I—" Itale sighed, draping a hand across his face. Embarrassment colored his cheeks, and he chastised himself for being such a fool. "It's been a while." Not that he hadn't taken lovers before, but intimacy had always been messy for him. Something about Tantien made him fearful of fucking it up.

"Itale." Itale raised his hand as Tantien ascended, and his fingers moved to cup Itale's cheeks. "We can move as slowly as you'd like. There's ah," Tantien laughed, a breathless exhale of air that brushed Itale's face. "There's something different about you. If I need to kiss every inch of your skin to prove how beautiful you are, I will."

Itale had no reason to think Tantien would be disgusted by him, but his heart was a fickle thing, betraying him. He still felt like a stranger in his own skin at times, felt like he haunted the halls of his bones.

"I think I have a better idea," Itale whispered, pushing gently against Tantien's chest.

Tantien's gaze turned questioning, but Itale ignored it, and Tantien allowed him to guide him back until Tantien lay on his back in nothing but his pants. Itale's mouth dried as his gaze trailed over all of the hard lines and pathways of Tantien's chest, the dip of his hips, the fabric pitched at his groin.

"Don't move," he demanded, and Tantien hitched a breath and nodded wordlessly, his fingers pressing into the cave floor as Itale scooted closer. His heart was in his throat, his desire an inferno in his belly as his hands found the edge of Tantien's pants and he pulled them off, followed hurriedly by his own.

He was in control. He had the power over Tantien, and it was exhilarating. It chased away his dysphoria as he straddled Tantien's waist.

Let go. Let go.

His desire sang such a mantra in his mind, so he did.

He let go.

TWELVE
TANTIEN

The sun rose too quickly for Tantien's liking. The rays washed away the threat of rain and danced in the remaining droplets that clung to the trees, and he woke first, his arm tucked over Itale's waist as he spooned him from behind. Itale was so cold that Tantien feared something was wrong at first, but as he rose his head, he was relieved to feel the steady rise and fall of Itale's chest as they lay close to the fire that had long since gone out. It was still warm beneath the plethora of furs he'd drawn over themselves after their intimacy the night before. Tantien contented himself with staying right where he was, his belly clenching mercilessly at the memory of Itale running his hands over Tantien's chest, his mouth descending to wrap around his...

"We have to go," Itale gasped, jerking awake. "Delroy is in danger." He scrambled away, his expression dazed and confused as Tantien straightened, the furs pooling at his waist.

"What do you mean? How do you know?"

Itale gave him a frightened look, his curls a disarray as he searched the cave for his clothes. There was no mention of the night they'd shared, no nod towards how Itale was feeling as he tugged his pants back on and shivered violently against the chill in the air. "You have to trust me. My necromancy, it—I just *know*."

Tantien nodded and hurried to his feet, finding his own clothes with ease. His joints were stiff from the cold, and he felt sluggish, as all eldrasi did when they were forced into colder climates. Still, the fear over Delroy's safety chased away his misery as they gathered up their things and hurried out of the cave. "We just need to get somewhere with enough space for Kalíra to land."

"We need to hurry." Itale's eyes were stained with tears. "I don't think we're going to get there in time."

Fear sang through Tantien, accompanied by guilt. It had been his decision to flee the Firebrand and seek out his grandfather, who wasn't even on the island. This had been a fool's errand.

And oh, what a fool he was.

They made it back to the beach, and Tantien called out for Kalíra, the song call haunting as a thick fog sank over the island. The seas looked calm today as Kalíra sailed overhead, dipping beneath the clouds to land nearby. He chirped, obviously in a manner of distress, and his wings appeared ruffled, like he had fared the worst of the storm.

Tantien pressed a gentle hand to the side of Kalíra's neck as he helped Itale up into the saddle and then swung up himself. There was no time for conversation, no time for expressing worry. He clicked his tongue against the roof of his mouth, and Kalíra took off, flying back towards the direction his crew and Delroy had gone.

He had to hope that Itale was wrong and they weren't too late.

The sun beat down heavily upon Tantien's head as Kalíra landed roughly, spurred to unease by Tantien's anxieties. There was something wrong. The Crimson Nightshade was anchored next to the Firebrand, but there was no movement from either ship.

"I don't sense any vampiric presence on the ship," Itale said, a worried expression on his face. It matched the growing pit forming in Tantien's belly. "I don't sense anything at all. No life, no death, nothing." Itale stared at his hands. "It's as if my magic does not exist."

"I feel it too." Tantien's magic had never been anything to praise, not like his sister's, but he had it enough to know when it wasn't there, and its absence was strange, like his veins ran cold. He shivered. "Come on. We need to find Delroy."

They walked in silence, the sand kicking up around his ankles as he studied the forest before him. It looked much the same as the one they'd just left, only it was as if something was lying in wait inside, a thickened trepidation in the air that rattled his nerves.

Tantien, you're such a fool.

His guilt weighed heavily as he forced himself forward, his fingers falling to his side to pry his hammer free of where it rested at his hip. Something was wrong. Could he have prevented it, had he not let his self-loathing and desire for revenge get in the way of their mission? He didn't know, but as they pushed further and further into the forest, the trees seemed to bend and reach out to cling to his armor, and he somehow knew they were walking into danger.

Come.

He stilled as the voice caressed him, as he shivered with anticipation.

Come find us, Welder of Flames.

A high-pitched noise pierced the air, echoing out through the trees, and Itale flinched beside him, his hands reaching up to clamp over his ears. Tantien instinctively moved closer to Itale, shielding him from whatever hidden dangers there might be in the trees, and he frowned.

"Stay behind me, *daumïr*," he demanded. He no longer sensed the trees of his homeland as if they were a second heartbeat, not since his grandfather had cursed their family, but he didn't need to perceive the trees' intentions to know that something was coming for them.

"Duck!" He turned, bending his body around Itale as he pressed them both to the ground, grunting in pain as something sharp slid across his back. *Keep Itale safe.* He had never felt so protective of someone before, but it consumed his mind now. Even as the uncertainty of Delroy's fate lay just out of reach, all Tantien could think of was calming the trembling man beneath him, of taking him back to the Firebrand where it was safer.

He looked up, but whatever had struck him was gone.

"Tantien, you're bleeding," Itale said softly, his fingers reaching up to graze Tantien's chin. "I can smell it, like a sickeningly sweet and sharp scent. Strange—I wasn't able to do that before..."

"I'm fine," Tantien said. "We need to keep moving. Did you sense anything just then?" He looked down and caught Itale's gaze, saw the same worry in Itale's eyes that plucked at his own belly.

"No. Nothing at all."

Threading Itale's fingers through his, he inhaled sharply. "Not even Delroy?"

Itale stilled, then closed his eyes. "Wait...I think I can. It's faint, but the rot of undeath is there..." he used his free hand to point. "That way."

Pain smarted at Tantien's back, but it wasn't so excruciating that it couldn't be ignored as they made their way through the forest. They stilled every so often as a twig snapped nearby, waiting until the world grew silent again before moving forward.

Tantien did not let go of Itale's hand, and Itale did not try to pull away, gripping his fingers so tightly they ached. Somehow, that anchor still didn't feel like it would be enough.

"Up there," Itale whispered after several minutes of walking. Nothing else challenged them, and the back of Tantien's back tingled as his wounds closed. His instincts were urging him back, cautioning him towards moving forward, but he ignored it, ignored the way it clawed at him. He didn't want to move forward as the air thickened and Itale shuddered beside him. The trees were still, as if they held their breath, the wind absent as silence strangled the air.

Itale cocked his head to the side and halted. "Wait. Tantien, I don't think it—"

The world went dark, as if something had snuffed out the sun's light. Tantien blinked as Itale was wrangled from him, his heart a flurry of panic as he reached out, but he could not see, his toe slamming into something hard and unyielding as he stepped forward.

"Itale!" He cursed as no response was given, and he reached out blindly, his fingers brushing against the trunk of a tree. So he was still in the forest. But where was Itale?

"Tantien." A voice sighed against his ear, accompanied by the brush of feather-light touches at his shoulder, and he lashed out with his hammer. It hit a tree, and the contact jarred him so much that his arm ached, his heart in his throat. Immediately, his fire was beckoned forth in his free palm, burning his fingers as he flung it away.

Laughter sounded behind him, and he cried out as pain flared up in his leg, the warmth of his sap-blood running down his calf. His frustration overpowered the pain he was in, his back screaming from the wound he'd received earlier.

Calm down.

His sister was the rash one, fueled by emotion. Tantien stilled and shut his eyes, forcing his breathing to calm. He recalled what Helai had told Linda once, about the importance of using every sense to see. If he couldn't see with his eyes, he'd use his ears.

Except everything had gone silent. Dark and silent. If he didn't feel the earth beneath him, didn't feel the soft caress of the wind against his skin, he might have thought he was dead.

Tightening the hold on the hilt of his hammer, he nudged his way forward. Surely this was some trickery, a magic birthed from witchcraft. He just needed to move beyond the magic, and then he needed to find Itale. He refused to entertain the idea that something horrible had happened to him.

Using his foot, he continued to nudge forward, but the magic refused to relent, and every once in a while, something would lash out and strike him. He never seemed to catch it, no matter how many times he lashed out with his hammer or his fire magic. Soon, several minor wounds welled from his arms and legs.

"If you're going to kill me, stop *fucking* around and do it already," Tantien growled, slumping against a tree. The pain was insistent now, a pulsing, scratching sensation that demanded his attention.

"Come and see him." A woman's voice echoed through his head, soft and tempting. "Come, come." Tantien didn't have a chance to speak before something swept him away.

When he came to, his sight had returned. He wished it hadn't, though. A blanket of snow covered the trees, giving the world an air of calm even though it was anything but. Shadowy demonic dogs wove through the trees up to their masters, men tucked behind deer skull masks. The trees were dark and imposing, and Tantien blinked snowflakes from his eyes as they fell upon Delroy, who was chained to the ground before the massive skull of a dragon. Beside him was a man Tantien did not recognize, and Zulthraine Kindroth, his grandfather.

The moment his eyes fell on his grandfather, a sickening anger swept through him. He had been hunting Zulthraine Kindroth for so long that now that he was here, he didn't know how to react. Zulthraine was tall, taller than Tantien, and leaner, with the same sweeping dark red hair and intimidating expression. Everything about him was sharper, and he was perhaps the most cursed of them all; the only indication of his eldrasian roots *was* the sharpness of his ears. Everything else was human-like, painfully so.

"Grandfather." He didn't recognize his own voice. He nearly didn't even hear it beyond the roar of rage echoing in his ears as he strained against the restraints that tied him to the tree. His grandfather ignored him, and some unholy thing liberated itself from Tantien's throat and shot past his lips.

"Zulthraine Kindroth. You *will* acknowledge me!"

His grandfather did turn then, his gaze burning into Tantien's. As he did, so did all of the cultists, their bodies angling towards Tantien, whose chest heaved in anger. He was aflame with it, and it was by some cruelness that he was confined to this tree; if only he could charge forward and feel his grandfather's skull crush beneath the weight of his hammer, or he could burn him alive in some sick, satisfied honor to his sister.

"I've been hearing stories of your pursuit for some time, dear grandson. I must admit, it wounds me, how angry you are. As if the weight of your conscious is my fault."

"The weight of my conscious?" Tantien scoffed, a cruel noise that echoed in the hollow of his throat. "*My conscious*? Untie me, so I can clear my conscious with the knowledge that I have buried my hammer into your head."

Zulthraine laughed. "I think not, Tantien. There are much bigger things at work here, and our family troubles will only get in the way."

The rope that bound him to the tree scraped against his wrists as he tugged against it. Delroy met his gaze, and for the first time, Tantien saw fear in the vampire's eyes. It reflected in Tantien's belly; he remembered the tales the Misfits had spun, recollections of a similar ritual beneath the Welker Estate, recalled how Cassius had spoken of his own sacrifice to resurrect Rhavna.

Was this the same sort of ritual? Was Delroy in the same danger Cassius had been?

Tantien's skin crawled as a shadowy dog drew too close, the red of its eyes glaring against the black smoke of its fur. It snarled up at him, white teeth gleaming, and Tantien repressed the urge to draw lips back over teeth in response.

"Delroy," he called out, turning his attention back to the vampire. "We'll figure this out, my friend. Do not despair."

Delroy grinned and tilted his chin up as the stranger next to Zulthraine approached. "Ah, but da secret of vampirism is simple: I made da peace with death long ago. I do not fear it."

"You should," the stranger said. In the light, Tantien realized it was Navaes, an eldrasi that Tantien hadn't seen since he was a boy. He had reason to believe he was dead, only he stood very much alive now. His skin was peppered with decay, like he had stood too close to something rotting. His hair was pitch black and dirty, hanging around his face and shoulders beneath a hat similar to Delroy's. Pointed ears jutted out from between his hair, and when he smiled, his canines were pointed, like a vampire's. Impossible, though. Eldrasi couldn't be vampires; the vampiric curse only infected humans.

Navaes leaned close and whispered something to Delroy, something Tantien could not hear. Tantien's gaze flickered about; he couldn't see Itale, which caused relief and terror to war inside him.

He was either safe or dead, and he didn't want to entertain the possibility of the latter.

"Children of Motaumr, come closer." Zulthraine raised his hands as the cultists shuffled forward. Off to Tantien's right, the brush shuffled and the wind brushed against his face. His head ached, like he had been struck. "Navaes wields the honor of returning one of our dearly departed to us this fine night, but we must steel ourselves against our fear. The sacrifice made here today will be written into the songs of those who are worthy enough to see the new world we are building." His gaze flickered, meeting Tantien's.

"Fuck the gods who scorn us. They sit upon their thrones and mock us, when they should be *serving* us. Let us welcome the True Gods and raise this one to aid us in the coming war."

"You're all fools," Delroy seethed. "Da Misfits will stop you."

Zulthraine and Navaes laughed, and it echoed throughout the clearing, haunting and low. "I have heard of these *Misfits*." Zulthraine spat their name like it was venom and bitter in his mouth. "I do not worry about their efforts, for they are folly." Turning to Navaes, he nodded. "It's time. I grow tired of waiting."

THIRTEEN
ITALE

Itale trembled in the cover of his hiding spot.

Death soaked the air so heavily that Itale could scarcely breathe; it clawed at his lungs and made his eyes water. He didn't know how he'd gotten away from the witch that had ripped him from Tantien's side, only that he'd come to, covered in her blood. There had been no time to wonder, no time to panic, as the forest was flooded with cultists who urged him to remain hidden by clinging to the trees and hiding in the brush. It was only after several panic-stricken moments that he found a perch in a bush where he could watch the scene before him unfold.

The clearing was massive, and somehow, the snow had all been dug or magicked away to reveal the darkness of the dirt underneath. Cultists stood, still as stone, peppered about as they all appeared before three figures and a massive dragon skull, similar to the ones the Misfits had described seeing in Rovania. Delroy was chained to the ground in front of the dragon skull, surrounded by Eldrasi identical in appearance to Tantien and a strange man who bore both Eldrasi and vampiric characteristics, which Itale didn't even know was possible. Tantien was tied to a tree across the clearing from Itale, and the moment he saw him, his heart thundered loudly in his chest, desperate to get closer. A flurry of movement near Delroy stole Itale's attention as the strange man raised a wicked dagger high above his head and then plunged it straight into Delroy's chest.

There was no time for words, no time for Delroy to say anything as black blood pooled up and burst from his lips. There was no time for much at all as Tantien's shouting cascaded over the clearing, and the rest of Delroy's men were slaughtered. Itale despaired, but he did not see any of the members of the Firebrand among the dead, and that gave him some small comfort.

Itale clung to the trunk of the tree in front of him, praying to whatever god might be listening that one of those shadow dogs did not come near him. He needed to think, needed to figure out a way to Tantien without being seen. He envied the ease with which Helai slipped through the shadows; he'd give anything in that moment to be able to do that.

Many of the cultists were distracted as they collected Delroy's blood in a shallow bowl. Itale's heart broke for the vampire's death, but his mind brushed it away, eager to find out how to save Tantien. They needed to get out of here before something happened. This was how Rhavna's resurrection began. The Misfits had told him such. He did not want to see that dragon come back to life.

Still, he spared a glance up at the skull anyway. It radiated with a strange energy, like the magic was so wild and untamed it threatened to pull Itale's insides apart. He was repulsed by it, wanted to pry his gaze away as the cultists began to mark the skull with various strange symbols using Delroy's blood. Still, even in his disgust, there was a quiet admiration that pulled at the corners of his soul, tempting worship.

A foul smell rose up to meet him. Itale scrunched his nose up in disgust as he bent and slunk towards Tantien, hoping that the trees were covered enough from wandering eyes and that the cultists were too distracted if they weren't. Stray branches attempted to cling to his shirt, prying it from him as he walked by, but his eyes were trained on Tantien, who was breathing raggedly, his eyes burdened with rage.

Itale had seen that same look when he was torturing the Vykra from before, only this time it was directed at who Itale assumed was Tantien's grandfather.

Something shuffled off to Itale's right, and he flinched left, taking care not to stumble into the clearing and break his cover. His foot hit a root, and he fell regardless, his head slipping into the clearing.

It didn't matter as the earth shuddered, the trees groaning as the air whistled with a swell of magic. Each cultist turned towards the dragon skull as Delroy's blood sank into the bone and disappeared. Then the world went silent, as if it were holding its breath. Nothing moved, and Itale stared up in horror as the skull shattered.

A living dragon was born from the fragments.

It unfurled as it grew, fabricated from the bones of its last mortal flesh. It was lean with a barrel chest, its wings long and thin with decay peppering the thin membrane. This dragon had four legs and a long claw on the tip of its wing for grabbing onto things, and its scales were a deep purple that reflected in the torchlight. Two horns spiraled out behind its head, with three sets of eyes that glittered like black gems as its opened maw revealed sharp teeth.

Itale's breath caught as the dragon raised its head and let out an earth-shattering roar. Purple flames cascaded from its open maw, heating the air as it kneaded the ground beneath its claws. Several of the cultists fell to their knees and pressed their foreheads to the ground in worship. Unlike the Misfits' recount of Rhavna's resurrection, this dragon did not burn or eat them. Rather, it settled, its wings drawing close to its sides as it snaked its head down and pushed its snout gently against Zulthraine's back.

"It is nice to see you again too, old friend."

Tantien locked eyes with Itale, his eyes widening in fear as they darted towards the treeline. *Get out,* his eyes pleaded. *Please save yourself before they see you.*

But Itale wouldn't. He couldn't, not without Tantien. He'd rip this entire island apart before they kept Tantien from him. He'd raise every dead thing long buried in the sand. He'd—

"What's this? A little rabbit strayed into a wolf's den where it doesn't belong?" Itale yelped in pain as someone grabbed him by the back of his shirt and yanked him roughly to his feet.

The clearing went silent as cold seeped through Itale's shirt and into his skin, a slow-crawling chill that he was too frightened to shudder from. The sharp edge of steel was pressed delicately to his neck, and he stilled.

"Navaes—I encourage you to think about what you're doing. I wouldn't want you to do anything...rash." Though Tantien's voice was calm, the anger that radiated from him was palpable, a tangible thing that slunk through the air like a slow-creeping fire.

"Strange. I haven't seen you since you were a young boy. It was once your sister's greatest joy to meddle in affairs not meant for her...have you taken up the task in her stead?" Navaes' voice rumbled against the back of Itale's head as he kept the knife poised against his neck, and Itale thought about how quickly it might take to kill him with necromancy. Would he be able to do it before Navaes killed him? Would he be able to do it *at all*?

"Does this boy mean something to you?" It was Zulthraine who spoke, his eyes blazing with contemplation as he stepped away from Tantien and approached Itale. There were glaring similarities between Tantien and his grandfather—both carried themselves with an arrogant confidence. Though Zulthraine's face bore sharper lines, there was no doubt that the two of them were related. Where there was kindness and amusement in Tantien's expression most of the time, however, Zulthraine's carried naught but anger.

Tantien's eyes flickered away from Itale, and he did not look at him again. "No. He's had some strange, sick fascination with me since he joined my crew some time ago, but I don't care for him."

The words struck Itale mercilessly. He *knew* Tantien was saying those things in a vain attempt to protect him, but they stung regardless. Stung worse than the blade at his neck. A strange whistling etched itself in the air, carried through the wind, and Itale's hands shook at his side as Navaes' laughter shook him.

"I don't believe him, Zulthraine. Maybe we should bleed him and see if your grandson talks."

"You could if you want, but Itale is the best necromancer I've ever come across. It would be foolish to bleed him when you could press him into servitude," Tantien said as Navaes dug the blade firmly into Itale's neck. A thin trail of blood ran down his skin, making him shiver. "It was why he was on my ship in the first place. Took out a lot of your men and used them to fight our cause." It was eerie how casually Tantien spoke, how carefully he tucked his anger behind indifference. Only Itale saw the twitch in his eye.

Zulthraine demanded attention as the dragon rose its head above Zulthraine's and stared down at Itale. "A necromancer, you say? And he's not a low vampire?"

Itale stared up at the dragon, too frightened to look away. It was incredible, like staring into the face of a god, and the compulsion to drop to his knees was almost overpowering as the dragon exhaled sharply, blowing hot air into Itale's face.

"No, but a high vampire said he has incredible talent with the magic. Killing him would be a shame. Just as killing me would be a shame."

The cultists had grown closer since the attention had turned away from the dragon's resurrection. They stood tall and silent behind their masks, as if they awaited command, and Zulthraine trailed closer to study Itale closely.

"My grandson is foolish and a terrible liar." Cupping Itale's chin, Itale felt the blade at his neck go away as Navaeas stepped back. Zulthraine's fingers were warm, warm like Tantien's, but they bore none of Tantien's kindness as he squeezed and tugged Itale closer. "You will wish he hadn't interfered. You will wish we had killed you before the end." Zulthraine glanced up and nodded, and Itale shuddered as his hand left Itale's chin. Navaes grabbed him again before he could dart away, and Zulthraine turned and gestured to one of the cultists as an echoing noise escaped the dragon's maw.

"The boy remains alive." The relief was tangible on Tantien's face as Naveas harshly twisted Itale's hands behind his back, causing him to yelp in pain. "But I'm afraid your deeds have gone unpunished for too long, grandson. The Phoenix Mother has whispered to me of your ventures with the Misfits, and lessons are long overdue." Zulthraine's eyes flickered to two of the cultists. "Bring him to me. We must bleed the corruption from him."

Itale's eyes darted nervously as two cultists moved towards Tantien, who remained silent as they cut away the rope that tied him to the tree. His heart was a symphony in his ears as the implications of Zulthraine's words set in. They were going to hurt Tantien.

"Stay still, little rabbit, before I decide bleeding you will please the gods more," Navaes whispered in Itale's ear.

Itale knew better than to tempt the patience of horrible men. Still, the cultists were bringing Tantien closer, where Zulthraine waited with his hands clasped behind his back. The dragon's impatience was felt, like a tangible thing in the air as it kneaded the ground and moved about at the edge of the clearing.

"Fight back, Tantien," Itale pleaded, wrenching himself away from Naveas' touch. The vampire's hands tightened their hold on Itale, and he despaired as he pleaded with Tantien. "Don't let them hurt you."

"It's alright," Tantien uttered. His smile was falsified, forged by the fear that lit up his eyes, and a tear rolled down Itale's cheek as they forced Tantien to his knees in front of Zulthraine. "It's alri—"

A resounding crack echoed against the trees as Tantien lolled to the side, and he whimpered. An angry, red welt formed on his cheek from where Zulthraine had slapped him, but he didn't give him a chance to recover before he descended upon Tantien.

Zulthraine showed him no mercy. Sap-blood flecked the snow as Zulthraine punched Tantien, who fell to the ground and attempted to cover his face from the wrath of his grandfather. A knife was pried from a sheath at Zulthraine's side, where he began to slice it across Tantien's skin. Itale pulled against Naveas despite the dangers, desperate to save Tantien from Zulthraine, but Naveas' hold was too strong, and a cry ripped itself from Itale's lungs as Tantien continued to refuse to fight back.

*No, no, no. You will not **take him from me.***

Something inside Itale broke, freeing the dam that welled inside his belly. The high-pitched screams of the dead echoed among the trees, but no one heard them but him as wind rustled the leaves and hinted at their approach. His hands grew bone cold, and Naveas shifted behind him as the dragon, suddenly unsettled, threw its head up and roared. Zulthraine seemed entranced by his beating, his blade a bloodied mess as it lashed out against Tantien's arms again, and again, and again...

Itale's eyes rolled into the back of his head, and everything went dark.

FOURTEEN
TANTIEN

Tantien floated in a sea of pain.

The ground was cold, violently so against his skin. Eldrasi were not equipped to deal with the bitter bite of winter, which was why Tantien always sought southern waters when the north hunkered down to prepare for its cold months. This cold was unnatural and did little to soothe the hurts that his grandfather inflicted upon him.

He didn't care. He had ensured Itale's safety, even if it was only for a few more moments. He couldn't bear the thought of watching him die. Some might call him a coward for it, but Itale was also *strong*. He'd figure a way out of this, even if Tantien didn't.

Tantien made peace with that. He'd been fighting for answers to his family's crimes for *so* long.

He'd finally be able to rest, but only if he could take his grandfather's life too. *Fight back, you fool*, he thought as he attempted to find the strength. *You've finally found him. Kill him.* His limbs refused to cooperate, though, beyond remaining near his face to keep Zulthraine's blade from striking his cheeks.

A sickening crunch echoed in the hollow of his chest as one of Zulthraine's boots struck out at his ribs. He wanted nothing more than to fight back. Igraine would have wanted him to fight back, but he couldn't. Not when Itale's life was in danger.

"Such a disappointment," Zulthraine seethed in between strikes. "Your parents would have been so disappointed to see their son now." A new flame was kindled, his words poking demons Tantien had long laid to rest. Tantien's parents were the source of a subject that the Kindroth siblings avoided. Their parents were deluded into thinking that the curse upon their name would simply...go away, given enough time. It sickened Tantien to see them ignore it so viciously.

His breath rattled. If his grandfather kept up at this pace, he wouldn't last much longer.

Just one more look.

His heart cried out for Itale; he hadn't had the chance to tell Itale how he really felt. Every exhale felt like fire in his lungs, every inhale rattling against the pain in his lungs. Perhaps it was for the best. Maybe it would make it easier for Itale to move on...

Just one more look.

The moment Zulthraine gave him a reprieve from his beating, he raised his aching head to peer up at Itale, whose arms were twisted and held against his back by Navaes. They had not harmed him, not that Tantien could see, and that relief was enough for Tantien to lay his head back down. Now he could accept his fate.

But something was wrong.

The air had gone still. Where there was once a chilling, biting wind, there was now an eerie stillness. A low whine curled against the trees, and Tantien shivered violently as the edges of his vision darkened. Gods, he just wanted to rest.

"Something stirs in the darkness," someone whispered. "The ghosts of this island waken."

"What's wrong with him?" Another voice said.

Tantien felt his grandfather move away from him, and he winced as he curled in on himself; one of his ribs was definitely broken, his arms a ruined mess from the wrath of Zulthraine's blade.

"He's calling all of the dead here. We need to get him to stop. Get him to stop immediately!"

Tantien's eyes flung open as Itale inhaled sharply, and his eyes shone with a vibrant, white light. Black veins edged his face and snaked along his arms and legs as a skeletal arm pierced up from the ground and grabbed Naveas' leg. A spirit, a transparent ghostly apparition, sailed through the trees, accompanied by many others as they drew close to Itale's side, as their pale, translucent fingers gripped at the cultists' masks. Zulthraine had reached the dragon's side.

"Navaes, leave them. We have succeeded here tonight. What is important is that we leave with the blade and Arvias. *Come.*" Tantien clawed through the snow to reach his grandfather as he maneuvered up the side of the dragon and swung onto his back. A wave of spirits screeched through the air, drawing any semblance of warmth that had existed as they clawed at the dragon's sides. The clearing had fallen to chaos as corpses rose from where they had long been dead, their skeletal remains ripping cultists apart. One cultist screamed as spectral hands pried their mask away and plucked out their eye, only to shove their fingers down the cultist's throat to silence them.

Zulthraine ignored them as the dragon shook away the ghosts, and Navaes raised his hand in panic and moved to stab Itale with the blade he'd killed Delroy with.

"No," Tantien whispered. "No..." Panic swelled in his throat as he forced himself to his knees, ignoring the screaming pain of his body and cursing at how slowly it was causing him to move. He needed to keep Itale safe. He needed...

A cry of pain shot throughout the clearing, and Tantien's head shot up. A bloodied stump sat where Navaes' hand once was, and Itale slumped to the ground as Navaes let him go with his other hand. Next to Itale's head was Navaes' disconnected hand, the blade they had traveled north to seek still curled delicately within his fingers.

A whoosh of air passed through the clearing violently as the dragon flapped its wings and took off, passing over the clearing low enough to grab Navaes with one of its feet. The dragon soared off into the night as Tantien dragged himself over to Itale. The cold seeped into his bones and stiffened his joints as the snow collected against his skin. Ignoring his pain, even as it tried to steal consciousness from him, he tugged Itale against him.

"Stay with me, *daumïr*," he rasped, wiping Itale's curls from his face. The ghosts, no longer sensing any threats, slipped away, leaving Tantien and Itale alone in a field with the corpses of cultists littered about them. Blood drenched the snow as Tantien stared down and flattened his palm against Itale's chest. He wasn't breathing, and Tantien's fear flourished. "Don't leave me. Not when I've just found you."

Sap-blood covered Itale's skin as Tantien's wounds wept, but Tantien pulled Itale closer regardless. The man in his arms was bone cold, his lips mottled with specks of blood, and Tantien was about to despair when Itale inhaled sharply, taking a glorious breath of air as his eyes shot open.

"Oh, thank the gods," Tantien whispered, pressing his lips to the porcelain of Itale's cheek. "I thought you'd died before I could tell you—"

Darkness came for him.

FIFTEEN
ITALE

A shuddered breath woke him from troubled sleep. It was dark, and the soft sway made Itale believe he was on a ship, though that was impossible.

His mind was disjointed, an echo of confusion that threatened to swallow him up as he rose from the bed he was in. Where was he? What had happened? He couldn't remember...

"Oh, oh *gods*," he groaned, raising his hand to his head. A headache pounded mercilessly against his skull with a heartbeat all its own, and his teeth chattered against each other as a chill took hold of him and refused to let go. It felt as if Death themself had knocked on his door and he'd nearly answered.

He *was* on a ship. The knowledge came to him slowly, slithering around his headache like a slow-crawling predator, and he looked about as he realized where he was.

Tantien's room.

It came flooding back all at once. The island. The cultists. Tantien's grandfather and the dragon — the dragon had been brought back. Itale's heart squeezed painfully. Delroy had never been close to someone he'd felt comfortable around, but his death weighed heavily on his mind. He couldn't imagine the turmoil that the news would put Rooster through.

"Itale?"

There was movement in front of him as Tantien stood from the chair behind his desk. Gauze bandages gleamed beneath his shirt and around his arms, and he walked with a slight limp as he made his way over to the bed. A soft noise etched his lips as he reached out to slip his fingers against Itale's cheek. He was just as warm as ever, and a relieved tear slipped from Itale's eye. The last thing he remembered was Zulthraine beating Tantien...he'd thought Tantien was going to die.

"You're awake," Tantien said, his voice so soft it nearly brought more tears to Itale's eyes. "I've never seen someone sleep for so long."

"How long?" Itale searched Tantien's gaze, struggling to stop himself from grabbing the front of Tantien's shirt and pulling him against him, where it was safe. The thought made him dizzy, still consumed by the headache that pierced his temple, and he whimpered quietly as he attempted to blink away the pain, his hand reaching up to clutch his forehead.

"Three days. I might have thought you a corpse had I not felt your breath on my cheek when I leaned down to see." Tantien's gaze softened. "I thought I'd lost you, *daumïr*."

Itale shivered at the pet name, and tears *did* come then. "There is no place you can go where I will not follow. I thought you'd know that by now. Same goes for leaving. I'm not going anywhere."

"You'd stopped breathing. When my grandfather..." Tantien swallowed slowly, collecting himself before continuing. "When my grandfather began to torture me, when the spirits showed up, none of that... I was so *frightened*. I've never been one for fear, but when I saw you slump over, when the spirits had gone and I dragged myself through the snow to you..." Tantien shuddered, and Itale reached a shaking hand up to rest over his. Tantien had always been *so* warm, a welcome relief to the aching chill in Itale's fingers. "I thought you had died before I told you."

Itale's stomach cartwheeled, his cheeks flaming as a slow smile worked its way to his lips. "Told me what?"

A curtain of red hair slipped from Tantien's shoulder as he leaned closer, his breath tickling Itale's face. Heat rolled off him in waves, and if he were in any pain, he didn't show it as he pressed a gentle kiss to Itale's forehead. It was such a raw, intimate gesture that Itale couldn't stop his body from trembling or his heart from threatening to burst from his chest. Something about Tantien unmade him.

"To the end of the world and the great beyond, I've been searching for someone like you, and I didn't even know it." Tantien pulled away to meet Itale's gaze once again. His nearness made Itale ache with want, as if his near-death experience was little more than a distant memory, a long-forgotten dream. "My soul may belong to the great tree of Daesthara, but my heart belongs to you, Itale. If you'll have it."

Pain forgotten, Itale reached up with his free hand to grip Tantien by the nape of his neck and pull him down, crashing his lips against his. Kissing Tantien was a liberation from all the pain and the sorrow of everything they had lost, every hurt and trial they'd just gone through. Kissing Tantien was like finally finding home, a warmth and comfort after searching for it for *so* long.

"I love you," he murmured against Tantien's lips, a soft shudder etched in his cheeks. "Gods, I love you." He'd spent his entire life feeling like he did not belong—his home in the Misfits had secured him that sense of belonging and more. He'd do *anything* to ensure its longevity. He'd kill an entire island of cultists over and over again if it meant he got to keep kissing Tantien and fighting to stop Rhavna and the gods from ripping this world apart.

Tantien pulled away, his gaze darting between Itale's eyes as a slow smile crawled onto his lips. He was so beautiful in that moment that Itale's breath hitched.

"I love you, too," Tantien said, his thumb stroking Itale's cheek. "Gods, if Igraine could see me now. She'd never believe it."

Itale laughed, and Tantien kissed him again. In that moment, Itale didn't care about knowing what had happened, whether they'd managed to get the dagger, or if anyone else was alive.

All that mattered was Tantien.

Kissing Tantien had been exhausting work, and Itale found himself drifting to sleep despite his aversions to it. He didn't want to stop, wanted Tantien to feel every ounce of love that Itale felt for him. Sleep did not care, and sometime later, he woke pressed to Tantien, the slow rise and fall of the eldrasi's chest a comfort he didn't want to move from. It was dark outside, but Tantien had lit the torches that lined the walls and the candles on the bedside tables, and the room was bathed in a gentle light that added to the comfort. Itale sighed, his fingers dancing along the bandages that wrapped Tantien's midsection.

"How are your wounds?" he asked. "I'm not hurting you, am I?"

"You could never hurt me, *daumïr*." Tantien brushed Itale's curls from his eyes when he lifted his head, and his gaze seared into Itale's when their eyes met. "They are wounds. They will heal. Eldrasi heal incredibly fast, if you give us time to soak up the sun. I'm more concerned about you."

"I'm fine," Itale protested, but in truth, he wasn't certain. There was something dead inside him, something that withered and died when he called out to the spirits to save Tantien. He knew necromancy was a hefty magic that demanded much; he could only be grateful it did not cost him his life. Still, there was much for him to learn. He'd need to seek out someone who knew more. Cassius had been a good teacher, but the vampire knight had no love for necromancy and could only teach Itale so much.

"You have plenty of time to rest while we journey back south," Tantien said, his fingers idly tracing pathways on Itale's face. There was sadness in his expression, and Itale's own gut twisted with grief.

"How many did we lose?"

Tantien took some time to answer. "Delroy's entire crew was sacrificed to Zulthraine's dragon. Sollatso follows us now, but I can tell she is grieving. She has refused to leave the waters near our ship even to hunt. As for the Firebrand's crew…" A sad smile graced his lips. "We suffered no casualties. I don't know where they were or what happened, but it was Arlaynia that found us. We have her to thank for rallying the crew and getting us safely back to the Firebrand." Itale tucked that information away; he'd have to seek out Arlaynia and thank her later.

"And the dagger?" Itale was almost afraid to ask. It's why they'd traveled to the north in the first place. There was no sign of Rhavna, but if they hadn't managed to get the dagger, all of the loss they'd suffered would have been for naught.

"Tucked safely away in my desk. It's got strange magic surrounding it. I'm urging everyone on the Firebrand to keep away from it for now," Tantien said.

"Oh, good." The relief was immense, but the victory was shadowed by everything else that had transpired. "Best we get that to the Misfits as quickly as possible."

Tantien hummed in response and then went silent.

"Are you okay?" Itale whispered, dancing his fingers over Tantien's chest. "I-I mean, if you don't want to talk—"

"I don't." Tantien's gaze heated, and Itale's stomach flip-flopped as desire flooded through him. "It will eat away at me though, if I don't." Rising, he urged Itale onto his back, kicked his leg over, and straddled Itale's waist. "This now, talk later," he promised, and before Itale could respond, Tantien leaned down and pressed a searing kiss to his lips.

Itale's hands slipped around to Tantien's back, demanding him closer, demanding he take up every inch of space between them. He attempted to retreat when Tantien winced, Itale's fingers drawing across a wound, but Tantien ignored it, his mouth pressing hot, wet kisses to Itale's jaw.

"Tantien, if you're hurt we should—" A soft moan left him as Tantien nipped at his neck, his fingers reaching down to slip beneath his pants and between his legs. His words were lost as Tantien's fingers teased him, as his tongue darted across the sensitive skin and he began to descend, stopping only to kiss the scars that marred the undersides of his breasts.

Itale let the current of desire carry him away from his pain.

SIXTEEN
ITALE

The euphoria from his orgasm had him twitching as Tantien lay pressed against him. Both men heaved, sweat collecting between them, and Itale's hand wove through Tantien's hair as they both reclaimed their breathing.

"I love you," Tantien whispered against Itale's neck, causing him to shiver. "I'll never stop loving you."

"What will the Misfits think?" Itale teased, breathless laughter escaping him. He missed the other Misfits dearly and would be lying to himself if he didn't say he was glad to be traveling back south. He hadn't asked Tantien yet, but he hoped they were sailing to meet them in Lyvira.

"Jealous things, surely." Tantien pulled himself out of Itale and rolled over on his back, a hand resting gently on his chest. Some of the gauze was stained with fresh blood, and Itale sat up, his brow furrowed.

"Where is some fresh gauze? Those need to be changed." After days and days of sleeping, Itale was anything but tired. Any weakness he still felt from using so much necromancy was ignored as he pushed the blanket off and stood. His state of nakedness was noted but also ignored, even as he felt the heat of Tantien's stare, and he padded towards Tantien's desk.

"Bottom drawer, right side. I had Alvae stock some in here just in case."

The room was cold against Itale's bare skin as he bent and pulled open the drawer, grabbing the gauze. He halted, noting a small bottle alongside it, and he gently pulled it out as well, his eyes finding Tantien's.

"That's yours. Don't ask how I managed to get all of the ingredients. It wasn't easy." Tantien laughed, and Itale's eyes flooded with tears. It was the potion he needed to aid in his transition. Tantien, despite all that they were going through, had ensured its creation to make sure Itale received it.

"I cannot—"

"You don't have to say anything, my love. Come here."

Itale did as Tantien asked, weaving around to stand next to him at the bed. He gripped the potion so tightly that he almost feared it would break or disappear; the gauze was in his other hand.

Tantien winced as he forced himself into a seated position, his hand pressed against his waist. There was more blood than there had been even just moments before, and Itale cursed silently. He should have been far more insistent on Tantien resting.

"Take that and then help me so that I can wrangle you back to this bed and refuse to let you leave it."

Itale smiled. After setting the gauze on the bed, he pulled the stopper from the vial and tilted his head back. The potion was as bitter as ever, and Itale grimaced as it slid down his throat, but he was happy. Happier than he'd ever been.

"Thank you, Tantien. Really. I don't know how you could have possibly gotten what I needed, especially with everything we've just gone through. I—" he took a deep breath, a successful attempt at reining in his emotions. "I am so grateful."

"It's only the start of repayment for saving my life," Tantien said quietly, shifting against the bed as Itale picked up the gauze again. "I did not think my grandfather..." It was Tantien's turn to steady his emotions, his lip trembling as his gaze hardened. "I did not think him capable of such monstrous things. He has always done terrible things believing them to be what's right for the eldrasi people, but to turn to the very gods my people loathe? It's beneath him. I'm uncertain what his goal is."

Itale was too distracted trying to peel the old gauze from Tantien's midsection without hurting him to respond immediately. Tantien hissed when the gauze pried off an old scab, and Itale stilled. He was no healer. He should have gone and found Alvae.

"I'm fine," Tantien assured, and after some hesitation, Itale continued until Tantien's midsection was bare.

Itale's breath caught; Tantien's chest and stomach were littered with weeping wounds, minor cuts that were accompanied by a few larger ones. All of them were shallow, as if to drag out the suffering, and a low whimper pressed against Itale's throat at the sight of them.

"This has to be so painful."

"You help distract me from the pain. In fact, I'm overdue for another distraction..." Tantien's fingers reached behind Itale to press against Itale's bare ass, and Itale laughed, swatting his hand away.

"Not until I've re-wrapped these wounds. At first light, I'm going to find Alvae so she can properly clean these. *Tantien*," Itale scolded as Tantien's fingers continued to tease. "We were talking about your grandfather."

Tantien's face instantly sobered, his hand pulling away to rest on the bed.

"You spoke of him and his intentions, but you haven't talked about what he did to you," Itale said, careful to approach the subject gently. "I'm sorry he did this to you." Itale's chest constricted at the reminder. It made him think of his own father, and the abuse he'd suffered at his hands.

"I've known for a very long time that my grandfather has lost his love for his grandchildren. It's something I mourned and accepted long ago. I'm more concerned with the fact that not only is he working with Navaes, but what he intends to do with the dragon he brought back and why there was no sight of Rhavna."

"Many questions. Many things to discuss with the Misfits, when we meet back up with them," Itale agreed, his fingers working to pull the gauze around Tantien. It was a shitty job, but Itale felt better than making Tantien sleep in the dirty gauze he'd been in before.

Tantien sighed, a hand rising to press against his face. "And tell Carter that Delroy is dead. I'm not certain how he'll take the news of his foster father's passing, but it won't be one I give lightly."

Itale wasn't certain either. He didn't know how he'd feel if *his* father died. Perhaps nothing at all. The idea of a father who loved him had died when he was a child.

"At least we have the dagger. It's something, for now," Itale said, tucking the last of the gauze away and patting Tantien lightly on the chest.

"Yes. One step closer to feeling like we have a chance against Rhavna and the gods, should any of them wake."

Itale shuddered. "I loathe to think of the possibility."

Tantien caught Itale's hand as he tried to pull it away. Raising it to his face, he pressed a soft kiss to each of Itale's black-tipped fingers, his gaze never once leaving Itale's. The gesture was so intimate that Itale's heart squeezed, and he darted forward to kiss Tantien.

He'd never grow tired of kissing Tantien.

"Let us not think of it anymore. We still have to get out of the dangers of northern waters, and we cannot speculate anymore until we've ensured the other Misfits have succeeded in keeping that god in Lyvira asleep," Tantien whispered, tugging Itale back into the bed.

"Kiss me until I tire of it," Itale begged, even though he knew he never would.

And so Tantien kissed him.

SEVENTEEN
TANTIEN

The sun rose with Itale in his arms, and despite all the pain that had transpired the last few days, Tantien had never known such peace.

He knew at some point he'd have to leave the safety of his bed. He'd have to confront the reality of what they'd learned and face his crew, knowing he'd left them to deal with the dangers of Rhavna's loyal. He'd failed them, and all he wanted to do was bury his face in Itale and never face his failures.

But he was the captain of the Firebrand, and good leaders weren't given a choice whether or not they wanted to face their own short-comings. Pressing a loving kiss to the top of Itale's sleeping head, he slowly slipped away, tugged a shirt and pants on, and left the safety of his room.

The forge was quiet, light filtering through the opening where Kalíra usually rested. The gryphon was absent, however, and despite the chill that wafted in through the opening, the sky was clear.

As he left the forge, he inhaled deeply, taking in the cold sea air. He'd need to see Alvae after speaking with the crew; his wounds ached, but he couldn't live with himself if he spent a moment longer avoiding the rest of the ship.

"Ely?" He stopped the first sailor he came into contact with, and the young eldrasi stopped and gave Tantien an even look devoid of emotion. Light bathed Ely's face in a soft glow.

"Yes captain?"

"Gather everyone on the top deck. I need to speak with you all. And—" he reached out to brush Ely's shoulder. "Even Yír. I want everyone in on this conversation." Ely nodded and shouted as he trailed the deck of the ship, and Tantien turned to climb up to the wheel, where Arlyania stood stoic and silent. He sensed her unease, and it clawed at him, a beast, one he refused to shy away from.

"Captain." Her tone was clipped as she adjusted the wheel and stared straight ahead. "Before you say anything and before the rest of the crew gets up here, I just want you to know... none of us blame you." While her fingers tightened against the wheel, her eyes softened.

"I would understand if you did." Honest words that slipped from him unbidden, and he leaned against the railing next to the wheel as the rest of the crew climbed the stairs and shuffled around Arlaynia and Tantien in a half-circle. Some remained on the stairs, and the only ones that seemed to be absent were Itale and the few they'd lost to the battles they'd faced in the recent days. Grief hung heavy in the air, now that they were given the proper time to do so, and all were silent as Tantien pushed off the railing and stood tall.

"I know it's foolish to think that I'm spared from your ire in the event of my recent absence, and I come to you with no excuses nor expectations of forgiveness. If any of you wish to depart this crew, know that you can do so without any resistance from me." He paused as the chill of the northern wind howled against the top deck, making him shiver. His wounds ached, ever the reminder of his grandfather's abuse. Still, he'd gladly bear them if only to nurture the guilt of abandoning his crew. "But know—if you decide to stay, I will never make the same mistake again. Not even when it comes to my grandfather."

Yír was the first to speak up, the flop of his ears tucked behind a black hankie as he took a long swig of the health potion in his flask. "We've already had a good talkin' about what all went on in the last few days and really, there's nothin' t' be said other than to ask if we're finally setting our sails back south? Th' crew has had enough of the north and I feel like me balls are going t' fall off any day now."

One of the sailors jabbed at Yír with his elbow. "You're a myr-lír...you don't have any balls!"

A resounding laughter echoed over the ship, and Tantien held up a hand to silence them. Where he was glad for their moment of merry and their easygoing forgiveness, grief clung to the air, a soft reminder that even though the Firebrand had persevered, the Crimson Nightshade and its crew of vampires did not.

"We must make sail for Lyvira. Delroy's sacrifice must not be in vain. The return of a dragon, even one so small as the one we saw ressurected, cannot go unchallenged, and the Misfits must be warned. If you are truly still with me, then our work is just beginning."

A somber silence encompassed them, the air thick with implications. The gods *were* returning, and if the cults succeeded, the world as they knew it would end.

"We're with you, Tantien." Arlaynia laid a hand on Tantien's shoulder, dragging him out of his spiral. "If you don't have anything else, go and see Alvae. You look like shit."

There was much he still wanted to say, but there would be time for that yet. They still sailed dangerous waters, and the faster they began their descent into the south, the better. So he nodded and waved his hands in dismissal. "Back to work then."

His crew dispersed without another word, and Tantien was grateful. Their unwavering loyalty was something he didn't deserve and would never take for granted again.

Tantien pressed his elbows to the railing of his ship and sighed as he stared out at a sea that bred the illusion of calm.

It was almost as if the terrors of that island had never happened.

But they did, Tantien chastised himself. *I mustn't forget.*

He'd find his grandfather and make him pay for all of the pain he'd caused Tantien and Igraine. Make him pay for the suffering of their people. Make him pay for nearly killing Itale.

"Tantien?" Itale's voice called out to him, and he turned his head as Itale sidled up next to him, sleep still stitched into his expression. There was a slight smile on his face, though, one that filled Tantien's chest with warmth, and Tantien slung his arm across Itale's shoulders and pulled him close.

No matter what the gods and Rhavna had in store for them, they'd be ready. They had the dagger now.

Acknowledgements

First and foremost, I want to give *myself* a massive pat on the back for accomplishing this novella while I was also going through my first pregnancy. This pregnancy was not easy on me in the slightest, and I still managed to keep up with my writing. I am proud of myself, and glad this little novella was able to see its publication before my son arrived.

As always, thanks to Katie for being the soundboard to my ramblings when I need a reader's perspective. Beta reading for me has been a lifesaver! Same to my sister, who has a closer relationship with the Misfits and does a fantastic job helping me weave the best version of these characters and their story. Thanks to my husband, who helps me out of writer's block when it strikes at the worst possible times, and for generally being my biggest hype man. I would not be able to publish books or attend events without him!

And biggest of thanks to those who have been with the Misfits thus far. Your love for this story fuels the flames of their journey, and I couldn't be more grateful that I get to take you along their quest. We return to the main Misfits in book 4 of the *Whispered Tales series*, and I cannot wait to share more with you.

Until next time, Misfits.

WHERE TO NEXT?

If you enjoyed *Our Souls We Keep,* please consider leaving a review wherever you're most comfortable. If you would like to stay updated with Dugdale's publishing journey, consider following them on Instagram and/or TikTok: @jordandugdaleauthor or signing up for their newsletter at jordandugdale.com. The Misfits' journey is far from over; I cannot wait to take you along for their next adventure.